"Oh, yes, Stacey! You have a brother."

Alida's green eyes blazed with uncontrolled bitterness. Words spat from her tongue in a destructive torrent. "Or should I say half brother. And while you've enjoyed your father's devotion all your life, your little half brother hasn't known a father at all. But you wouldn't care about that, you want your father all to yourself. Well, you keep your father all to yourself!"

"Alida!" Shock was stamped on Gareth's face. "What the hell are you saying?"

"You have a son, Gareth!" she hurled at him. "A son you're never going to know. Because he is mine. And just as your daughter won't let me near you, I won't let you near him!"

Alida undid her seat belt, opened the door and got out of the car. She didn't look back.

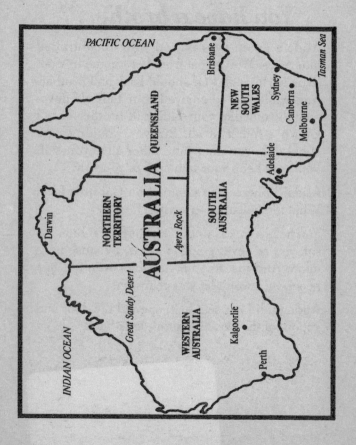

EMMA DARCY

Heart of the Outback

Harlequin Books

TORONTO • NEW YORK • LONDON
AMSTERDAM • PARIS • SYDNEY • HAMBURG
STOCKHOLM • ATHENS • TOKYO • MILAN
MADRID • WARSAW • BUDAPEST • AUCKLAND

Harlequin Presents first edition January 1993
ISBN 0-373-11519-9

HEART OF THE OUTBACK

CHAPTER ONE

"...ALIDA ROSE..."

Gareth's hand stilled on the bow tie he had been trying to fix to his satisfaction. It wasn't her. It couldn't be her. Not after all these years. Gareth's mind groped to remember exactly how many years it had been.

Perhaps he had misheard the name. His mind shied away from the memory conjured up as he shifted his gaze from his reflection in the mirror to the reflection of his daughter.

Stacey was sprawled across his bed, the evening newspaper spread around her as she gleefully read out the article that described what he had to suffer through tonight. Other names spilled from her lips, a list of who's who in the fashion world, all vying for the coveted award of Australian Designer of the Year. Surely to God he had misheard *that name!*

It would be penitence enough to sit through an inane parade of ridiculous clothes. He didn't need the added torture of seeing the one woman who would inevitably remind him of his most grievous sin. He had been through enough hell, carrying the burden of that secret guilt.

Stacey looked up, caught his eyes and grinned. The bright vitality of her thirteen-year-old face poignantly recalled the image of her mother, the woman he had loved and married, the woman whose love had been big enough to offer him sexual freedom when disease had rendered her incapable of functioning as a woman.

The idea of loveless sex had been repugnant to Gareth after what he and Kate had shared together. He hadn't sought to relieve his enforced celibacy. Yet when temptation had come at an opportune time... He still hated himself for having succumbed to the need that had overwhelmed all his finer instincts.

There had been something compelling about Alida Rose. From the moment they met he had wanted her. She had wanted him, too. But that was no excuse for losing all control, for feeling things he had never felt with Kate. It had been a betrayal of his marriage, not a simple, easily dismissed surrender of a sexual drive that he had all but forgotten in caring for his crippled wife.

And Alida Rose had been so hard to forget, a torment of loss to add to his guilt. Madness to feel what he had in the face of who and what she was. A city woman. A dress designer committed to superficialities. While Kate, the true partner of his life...

"You're really going to hate this, Dad," Stacey declared, her dark eyes dancing teasingly, unaware she echoed his uncomfortable thoughts.

"Yes, I expect I shall," he replied grimly, then tried to shake off his preoccupation with the past. Kate was at peace now. Nothing could hurt her any more.

"They're going to have a rock band playing all night."

His grimace was one of pained resignation.

Stacey laughed, well aware of his preference for classical music. "You shouldn't have let Aunty Deb put the screws on you to take her. She's got plenty of friends. She doesn't really need you with her."

Much as he hated society gatherings, Gareth owed his sister too much to refuse her a favour when she asked. She had given invaluable support during Kate's last months, and now she had offered her home to Stacey for the duration of her secondary education. His visits to Perth were few enough. The least he could do was oblige his sister when he was here.

He forced his fingers to rework the bow tie into an acceptable state as he answered his daughter. "Deb wanted an official escort. I doubt your uncle Max would approve of her taking any other man. And since he's in New Zealand on business..."

Stacey made a scoffing sound. "That's her excuse, Dad. Uncle Max didn't want to go, and so he went to New Zealand. That gave Aunty Deb her opportunity. If you ask me, Aunty Deb just wants to show you off. Even the girls at school think you're pretty hot stuff."

He frowned at Stacey. Her language was starting to deteriorate. *Put the screws on* belatedly registered in his mind. Now *hot stuff!* "What's that supposed to mean?" he queried disapprovingly.

Kate wouldn't have liked to hear their daughter speaking like that. She had always been so keen on Stacey getting a proper education. Even though they could well afford to employ a governess, Kate had preferred to supervise Stacey's correspondence lessons herself. Now it seemed all her insistence on good expression was being eroded.

Stacey heaved a sigh as though he was the backward student. "You know, too hot to handle. That kind of thing. That's how *they* talk. I have it on good authority that you're a cross between Cary Grant and Clint Eastwood. Some girls are stupid. But that's how they think. They say you have Paul Newman eyes, too."

"Good God!" He was appalled to think of his daughter's friends discussing him in such terms. "Is this the education you get at an exclusive school for young ladies?"

"Not from the teachers. But it's what most of the girls think of."

"I'll go and see the headmistress."

That got her attention. She swung her long pony legs off the bed and sat up, an anxious look on her face. "Dad, please don't cause trouble."

"No trouble."

She took his double meaning and saw there was going to be plenty of trouble. "Dad, it's the same everywhere," Stacey put in desperately, anxious to extend *his* education. "The school you and Aunty Deb think so highly of is a hotbed of repression. All the private boarding schools are. We play sport with the other schools, so I know they're the same. All the girls talk about is sexual fantasies and stuff like that."

"Don't you think it should be stopped?"

"Going to the headmistress isn't going to stop it, Dad," she warned him with a wise look.

He noticed the slight bumps of budding breasts pressing against the soft cotton T-shirt she wore with her jeans. She had only just turned thirteen. Did it happen so soon these days? Was he hopelessly out of date? What would Kate think of this?

Stacey's expression changed to one of appeal. "It is sort of interesting, you know."

"It should be stopped," he muttered grimly. "Crazy obsessive nonsense! They should be thinking about— well, sport and schoolwork and..."

"I don't have a mother to talk to about it."

That stopped him. Girls matured earlier than boys. He had to remember that. And with Stacey boarding at school during the weekdays, a whole lot of thirteen-year-olds together, reaching puberty, aware of the changes in their bodies, getting silly about it with no mature person around to give them a sense of proportion...

Teachers probably weren't the answer. And what good could he do? Stacey was only here at Deb's because he was in Perth and the headmistress understood their situation. Property owners like Gareth came down to Perth so infrequently that the schools gave them every opportunity to be with their children. Of course, Stacey had Deb to stay with on weekends. Couldn't his sister be a stand-in mother for her?

"Maybe your aunty Deb..."

Stacey sighed and looked askance. "It's not the same."

She was right. It wasn't the same. For twelve years she had been with him and Kate. Stacey had not yet forged any deep familiarity with his sister. No doubt Deb was involved in her own social activities on weekends, which left Stacey dependent on her school friends for company and confidences. If he made trouble for them, she could be ostracised from any friendship.

"I'll think about it," he said slowly. "Going to the headmistress, I mean."

Stacey's face lit with relief. Knowing she had won, she lay down on the bed again, propping pillows behind her head, resting content.

"Of course, the girls think you are impossibly romantic because you own a big cattle station in the Outback. That makes you a sort of macho king of the range."

He gave her a look of sheer disbelief.

Stacey grinned. "Well, Riordan River is in the Macdonnell Ranges." She attempted to look serious. "I think that's where the Clint Eastwood bit comes in, because he's a bit of a cowboy in a sort of way. And you're tall and strong-looking and..."

"Spare me school girl fantasies," Gareth muttered darkly.

"Well, you are my dad, Dad," Stacey assured him. "Most of the other girls' fathers are weeds compared to you. I must say I like having you as my dad."

"Thank you," he bit out.

"And then there's the attractive cleft in your chin."

"It's a darned nuisance when I'm shaving!"

Stacey ignored his irritable protest. "That's the Cary Grant bit. And having such blue eyes with your black hair and darkly tanned skin..."

"Haven't your friends got better things to do than to dissect me into movie actors' parts?" he rasped in exasperation. "What's on your list for homework?"

"That's it, you see!" Stacey said triumphantly, bouncing up to sit hugging her knees. Cunning gleamed in her vibrant dark eyes as she pursued her argument. "I know Aunty Deb talked you into placing me at Heatherton because it's her old school, and it's socially advantageous—" she wrinkled her nose in disgust "—but I'd be much better off at a normal co-ed high school where—"

"There are boys," he finished dryly.

"I'm used to being with boys. I've been with boys all my life. And they're a lot more fun than stupid girls. They're not always talking about clothes and make-up and looking sexy." She pouted in a travesty of nymphet sexiness.

"Stacey." Gareth sighed and swung around to face her. "Give it time, sweetheart. You've lived an isolated, narrow kind of life on the station. I know this is a different kind of world for you. But it's part of life, too. Country, city...it's best that you experience both so when you're old enough to choose what will most satisfy you, you can cope with whatever you have to meet."

Her face fell. Her dark eyes pleaded with his. "I hate it here. I want to be on the station with you, Dad. And when you're dead, I'm going to run it."

His loneliness sent a surge of empathy through him. Yet he had to resist it for Stacey's own good. He didn't like the way her education was being broadened at the present moment, but broadened it had to be. His daughter—Kate's daughter—was going to develop all her capabilities and become a well-rounded person whether she liked it or not.

"Stacey, Deb hated being away, too, when she was your age," he said quietly, and he hoped persuasively.

"But I don't want to become a socialite," she argued mutinously. "It's stupid!"

"Tell me that when you're eighteen, Stacey. Then you will have fulfilled your mother's plan for you and the choice will be yours."

"But that's five more years, Dad," she wailed.

"I know." An ironic smile curved his lips. "Almost a lifetime. Let's see now. In a couple of more years, I will have lived eight spans of five years."

"Yes." She glowered at him for being amused. "And Aunty Deb says you're getting all dried up."

He cocked an eyebrow in arch inquiry. "Does she now?" He reached back and picked up his empty glass from the dressing table. "Well, perhaps you'd be so kind as to pour your old dad another drink."

She huffed and swung herself off the bed, giving him a look of exasperation as she stood up and flicked back her thick black plaits. "Aunty Deb says you drink too much, too."

"I'm beginning to think Aunty Deb has far too much to say."

"I heard her tell Uncle Max that you're deadening your natural urges with the whisky bottle. So it can't be good for you," Stacey warned seriously.

His face tightened. His sister obviously needed a lesson in discretion. She spoke altogether too freely in front of his daughter. "I'll be the judge of that, Stacey," he said with a curtness that brooked no argument.

"If you say so, Dad," she said uncertainly, giving him a worried look as she took the glass from his hand. "She also said it's time you stopped being a eunuch. What's a eunuch, Dad? Aunty Deb wouldn't tell me, and Uncle Max went all red as though he was going to explode when I asked him. I tried looking it up in the dictionary but I couldn't find it."

Gareth gritted his teeth. He was going to give Deb one hell of a talking-to tonight. "The same as a gelding, Stacey,'' he answered in terms she readily understood.

''Oh! No good for mating anymore.'' She digested the concept then cast a curious look at him.

''I assure you I'm fully intact and perfectly capable of anything I so desire,'' he stated defensively.

''Do you?''

''Do I what?''

She grimaced at his slowness. ''You know. Desire anybody.''

He swore under his breath. Stacey was growing up too damned fast under his sister's wing. Not to mention peer-group influence. ''I loved your mother, Stacey.''

''Yes, I know, Dad,'' she agreed gravely. ''But I can hardly remember when you slept together.''

''That was because...'' He sucked in a sharp breath. This was getting more complicated than he could handle. ''Damn it all!'' he burst out in frustration. ''This conversation is at an end. Would you mind getting me a drink while I finish dressing to your aunty Deb's requirements?''

''Sorry. I didn't mean to upset you over Mum,'' she said softly, shaming him with her understanding. ''I guess that's why you drink so much,'' she observed as she went out the door to do his bidding.

Gareth closed his eyes and shook his head. He knew precisely when he had started drinking with mind-numbing regularity. It had become habit now, but then... Then he had sought any means that might help him dull his senses, help him forget enough so that he could get to sleep at night.

He released a long shuddering breath, opened his eyes, stepped over to the bed and picked up the page of the newspaper that Stacey had been reading from. A quick cursory glance was enough to dismiss the doubt he had nursed. He hadn't misheard. The name leapt out at him.

Alida Rose.

So what if she was there tonight, he asked himself savagely. She didn't mean anything to him anymore. It had been finished when Kate had died. There was no point in thinking about Alida Rose. She had moved on and up in the world. He would soon be going back to his. They would merely be ships passing in the night, ships that had passed before, five years ago. As Stacey would say, a lifetime ago.

CHAPTER TWO

GARETH MORGAN!

Alida stared at him, feeling as though she had just been punched in the heart. Five years had not diminished the charismatic impact of the man. At this distance he didn't look a day older.

A sick kind of compulsion made her glance around the party of people who had accompanied him into the crowded ballroom. She recognised his sister, Deborah Hargreaves, one of Perth's leading socialites. There was no woman in a wheelchair. He had not brought his wife.

Alida wrenched her gaze away. Her whole body began to churn with turbulent emotions. Why was he here? Why did he have to turn up tonight of all nights? She had been feeling happy, excited at having her designs displayed in front of such a glittering collection of stars in the fashion world, and even secretly hopeful she might win the award. Reaching this pinnacle in her career was what she had dedicated most of her life to over the last five years. It was her future.

Seeing Gareth Morgan again made all she had worked for seem meaningless. And that was wrong!

She couldn't let him do this to her. Hadn't she been through enough hell because of him?

"Gareth Morgan!"

Alida struggled to control her reaction to Jill's surprised identification. She should have been prepared for it. Jill had been giving a wickedly witty commentary on everyone in the ballroom. The new arrivals were not about to miss her keen eye. As a publicity agent, Jill Masters prided herself on knowing everybody who was anybody, and she certainly knew Gareth Morgan.

All her companions around the table looked in the direction of Jill's gaze, all except Alida. She concentrated on pulling herself together to weather the conversation bound to follow.

"Which one?" Suzanne asked, avidly scanning the string of people who were undoubtedly being ushered to their table by now. Although Suzanne Day was Alida's work manager, she had not made that fateful trip to Riordan River with them. They had been cutting all unnecessary costs in those days.

"Escorting his sister, Deborah Hargreaves," Jill supplied.

They all knew the wife of Max Hargreaves. As he was one of Perth's more prominent entrepreneurs, Max Hargreaves was news. His wife liked to consider herself a trendsetter, and that made her news as well.

"That's Gareth Morgan?" Suzanne asked with awe.

"That's him," Jill affirmed.

Alida did her best to project a calm composure as both women turned their eyes to her. It was painfully obvious that her closest associates had talked about Gareth Morgan among themselves. Natural enough, she supposed, considering what had happened and how it had affected them. All of it could be dated to the time spent at Riordan River, and Jill had been there.

Jill Masters was no fool. Putting two and two together was child's play to her. Yet she had held her tongue where Alida's personal life was concerned. Discretion was an important asset in an agent, Alida thought appreciatively. Probably the most important.

"What a great hunk of macho man!" Ivan Poletti pronounced with admiring relish. "Lovely. Do tell me about him, Jill. Why haven't we seen him on the social scene if he's the delicious Deborah's brother?"

Alida tensed. Ivan adored gossip. He was Perth's most fashionable interior designer, a dynamic, robust little man with a flamboyant personality. His bright brown eyes gleamed expectantly as he waited to be enlightened.

"He owns and runs the Riordan River cattle station in the Macdonnell Ranges," Jill supplied matter-of-factly. "He used to attend operas and classical concerts many years ago. Then his wife developed some disease—multiple sclerosis, I think—and their life narrowed down to Riordan River."

"Sad," Ivan commented, trying to look socially mournful while not really caring. He was cogitating other things. "Riordan River. Why does that name seem familiar to me?" He raised his eyebrows questioningly.

Alida knew it would click any minute. Ivan Poletti had a mind like a ferret, sharp and darting and acquisitive. "We took some location shots there for our first catalogue," she said, trying to make it sound unimportant. "Jill arranged it."

"Yes. That was the catalogue that got our foot in the door," Jill said with a triumph grin. "All we needed was the right gimmick, and what better than Outback settings?"

Ivan raised a finger in acknowledgment. "I remember. Fabulous photographs." He turned his attention to the newcomers.

Alida couldn't. She had too many memories.

The Riordan River Station, Alida thought bitterly, one of the largest cattle stations in the world, measuring thousands of square miles in the red heart of Australia, and every mile of it owned by Gareth Morgan. If only Jill had told her he was married before they had gone there... Or if his wife had been at the homestead instead of having treatment in hospital... But would it have made any difference to how she had felt about Gareth?

The attraction had been compelling from the moment she had first seen him. It had clutched at her heart: that air of indomitable male who could endure any adversity, a face carved with strength and a hard austere beauty, hair as black as midnight, piercing blue eyes that saw the far horizons, skin perpetually tanned from a merciless sun. One look at him and she had been his, to take as he willed. Madness . . .

Alida tried to shake her mind free of him, concentrate on the life she had made hers. The conversation had moved on. Suzanne was telling her live-in boyfriend how the tourist boutiques on the East Coast had found Alida Rose Creations a bonanza for sales, and how the unique range of clothes had gradually become a top fashion line. It was Suzanne's job to see that all quotas got to market outlets on schedule. She was very good at it.

She was also a good friend. So was Jill. So was Ivan. Good, reliable friends. Although they only knew one side of her, the public side of Alida Rose who was on display tonight, not the Alida Rose Gareth Morgan had used without conscience because she was of the fashion world. And everyone knew that the fashion world had no morals.

She supposed if she was judged by her company tonight, she was damned on every score. Jill, a very sophisticated woman of forty odd years, had already discarded two husbands and was working on the third with her current lover. Yet as an agent, she had worked tirelessly and fruitfully to promote Alida's designs.

Suzanne was honest and trustworthy and dedicated to her job, but she was thirty-three and her private life was a mess. Her escort this evening was a toy-boy artist who lived off her.

As for Ivan, there was probably no more blatant homosexual in the city. He had an astute business brain and had persuaded Alida to branch out into fabric design. Ivan's companion, Jonathan Lee, owned a string of hairdressing salons, and had joyfully had his way with Alida's hair for tonight, styling it into a rippling mass of soft waves.

Perhaps they all had their own self-interest at heart in being her friends because she had served them well in their careers. Nevertheless, they had stood by her when Alida had needed their support. Whenever she had called upon them for anything, they had responded generously, and she would never forget that.

Yet they were city people. Not one of them understood what it was to be Outback born and bred. They thought her designs marvellous, but they had no appreciation of the life behind them. They would never understand what she had grown up with, the timeless link with land and nature so pervasive that it seeped into one's consciousness and stayed there forever.

Impossible to explain, and Alida didn't try. That was the private Alida Rose, the one who had been so overwhelmingly attracted to the man who had only seen her as a body.

Gareth Morgan hadn't recognised that knowledge in her, hadn't sensed the love they could have shared. His mind had not accepted anything beyond the fact she was a woman. And what was worse, a woman of modern fashion, with modern ideas and modern morals. Fair game for any man!

Why had he come here tonight? Why was he mixing with the kind of society he scorned? Was he simply obliging his sister by being her escort for the evening? It was through Deborah Hargreaves that Jill had arranged their visit to Riordan River for the location shots. He had obliged his sister then. And got what *he* wanted out of it. Perhaps he was obliging his sister now for the same purpose, scouting for another easy woman to take the edge off his needs.

The lights dimmed. A spotlight lit the compere as he strode across the stage to the microphone placed ready for him. For the next two hours the crowd in the ballroom was entertained by a fast-moving kaleidoscope of fashion designs mixed with top-level entertainment. It was a highly professional exhibition.

Alida appreciated it, yet she felt strangely numb. She clapped when she was supposed to. She responded to her friends' comments. But there was no stir of excitement inside her, not even when it came to the final announcement, the one she had been waiting for all night. She felt the rise of tension in her friends, knew that they wanted her to win. Somehow she couldn't bring herself to care.

"And the award, Australian Designer of the Year, goes to—" the compere paused for dramatic effect "—Alida Rose!"

Everyone at her table erupted with excitement, Suzanne with emotional tears in her eyes, Ivan clapping and shouting "Bravo!", Jill beaming triumph as she gave her characteristic thumbs-up sign.

Alida knew she should feel wildly elated. Apart from the tremendous honour of winning the much-coveted award, the resultant publicity would boost her recognition enormously and increase sales. Such acclaim from the fashion industry was certainly a hallmark in her career.

All evening, since seeing Gareth Morgan again, a flat emptiness had been growing inside her, and not even this moment of triumph erased it. She pasted a smile on her face and forced herself to her feet, acknowledging the thunderous applause from the ballroom.

Conscious of the television cameras and knowing commentators would be describing the action to viewers all around Australia, Alida concentrated on walking up to the stage with dignity and grace. Pride held her head high, not so much pride in her success, but the deep personal pride of showing Gareth Morgan that her life was perfectly complete without him.

It was a lie, of course. It had been a lie from the moment she had met him five years ago. But she would never let him know that.

Black is the colour of my heart, she thought savagely. It seemed very appropriate that she was wearing black tonight, although no-one else would see any significance it in. A ripple of ironic amusement ran through her mind as she imagined how the commentator would be describing her outfit.

"Alida Rose is wearing one of the elegant culotte suits she is so well-known for. The silk pants are a swirl of sensuous pleats. The figure-moulding vest—curves are definitely in this year—features the kind of border design that is the trademark of so many Alida Rose creations. Inspired by Aboriginal art, the intricate border pattern is depicted in a bold arrangement of gold, silver and amber beads."

She remembered some fanciful columnist had once described her long blond hair as rich caramel with streaks of melted butter, and her eyes the colour of still green pools. A serene, sensual beauty with warm golden skin, she had been called, but Alida felt no serenity tonight. As for sensuality, Gareth Morgan had killed that quality in her five years ago.

Was he watching her? Was he remembering how she had looked in the heat of passion? Or had there been too many women since then for him to recollect any personal details from one particular encounter?

It wasn't as if he had loved her. He had wanted her only as a release from sexual need. She would never, never forget the shame and humiliation she had felt on realising that was all she meant to him.

She fiercely wished he wasn't here, spoiling this night for her.

The applause gradually faded as she mounted the steps to the stage. The compere extended his hand to her, presenting her to the crowd. Spotlighted for all eyes, Alida increased the voltage of her smile. She was the winner, and winners always smiled. What they felt inside didn't matter.

The compere made a little ceremony of passing over the statuette before inviting her to the microphone. A sea of faces looked up at her from the packed ballroom. The cream of Perth's society had flocked here tonight to enjoy the glittering event. Not often did it take place in Western Australia. Almost invariably one of the capital cities on the East Coast hosted the yearly event. The applause had been all the more enthusiastic because one of their own, a Perth designer, had won the top award.

Alida didn't know where Gareth Morgan was seated. She didn't want to know. She didn't want to see him again. She fastened her gaze on the people at her table, the people who had helped her to this success, and gave her speech of thanks to them.

More applause accompanied her exit from the stage. Alida was intensely grateful to be out of the spotlight. Pride insisted she see this evening through to its end. Celebration was certainly in order, so celebrate she would, no matter how hollow it felt.

"Darling, I shall find the most perfect pedestal for that sweet, sweet statuette," Ivan declared the moment she returned to her table.

Alida cocked a teasing eyebrow at him. "A little pretentious, don't you think?"

"For you, dear girl—" he reached out and stroked the statuette in one of his extravagant gestures "—one is allowed to be pretentious."

"And since Ivan has proclaimed—" Jill chimed in.

"It would be *terrible* not to do it!" Suzanne finished.

Ivan's temperamental outbursts when his artistic eye was offended were legendary and had earned him the soubriquet of Ivan the Terrible. He relished the name, deliberately choosing to write under it when he did his titillating and scathing gossip column for the Sunday newspaper.

Suzanne's pun brought a general burst of laughter. All her friends were riding a high. Wit bubbled around the table along with the champagne Ivan had ordered. His flamboyant nature made him scintillating company, and Alida was content to sit back and watch him perform.

The evening wore on. Couples crowded onto the dance floor. People table hopped, commenting on the fashion display they had seen.

Alida did not move from her table. She did not want to risk an accidental meeting with Gareth Morgan. She did not want to acknowledge his presence in any shape or form. However, a great many people flocked to them. She didn't have to say much. Her boisterous friends were only too happy to fill in for any reticence on her part.

Jill resumed her running commentary on what was happening around them, who was with whom and why. Ivan gleefully embroidered on it with choice bits of gossip. They were both in top form, and Alida was amused out of her private introspection until Jill spoke the one name she did not want to hear.

"Gareth Morgan is moving purposefully towards us," she warned on an uncharacteristically sober note. "His radar antenna is definitely focused on you."

One sharp glance at Jill's shrewd eyes and Alida saw that her agent knew altogether too much. Yet there was a promise of support in her expression, as well.

"A courtesy call, I expect," Alida forced out flatly.

It could be nothing else, her mind dictated. There were people here who had seen the catalogue, knew of the connection. His sister had probably blabbed it to her party. Perhaps Gareth Morgan felt obliged to offer her congratulations on being given the top award tonight. Such a move from him, however, was totally unanticipated by Alida, and it threw her into emotional turmoil. Nevertheless, she managed to lift her glass of champagne to her lips with apparent unconcern. She needed a drink. Her mouth had gone as dry as the desert on which Gareth Morgan imposed his will.

She knew precisely when he came to a halt beside her. All her friends looked at him, various degrees of curious interest or speculation on their faces. She continued to sip the champagne until he addressed her.

"Alida." Soft and low, but resonant enough to undercut the noise around them and make her pulse throb in her temples.

She turned slowly and lifted her gaze to his, her green eyes cool and steady. "Gareth Morgan. How surprising to see you in such a milieu!'' she said with light mockery. ''But I'm not sure it doesn't suit you.'' She said it to hurt, and it did.

His mouth quirked in sardonic acknowledgment. The blue eyes gleamed with worldly cynicism. ''Not my usual stamping ground, I'll admit, but my sister makes efforts to civilise me from time to time,'' he replied easily. He nodded at the statuette on the table. ''Congratulations on your success, Alida.''

''Thank you.'' She nodded towards her publicity agent. ''You might remember Jill Masters? I owe much of my success to her and others.''

''Yes, of course I remember Jill. You must be very pleased with all the accolades tonight,'' he said with smooth urbanity.

He could don civilisation like a cloak, Alida thought. But that was all it was to him, a veneer that had its usefulness when it suited him. In the formal black dinner suit he wore, he looked every inch a man of supreme sophistication. Underneath the cloak was a raw barbarian, a total savage.

Some perverse pride goaded her to make him acknowledge every one of her friends. He handled the introductions she made around the table with grace and polish.

For once, Ivan did not make some titillating or outrageous comment. Alida didn't know if she was grateful or disappointed. It rather irked her that Gareth Morgan had the innate quality of commanding respect without so much as raising a finger. He didn't deserve it, she thought bitterly.

"It was kind of you to come out of your way to offer us congratulations, Gareth," she said dismissively, meeting his eyes once again with all the casual aplomb she could muster.

"I wanted to." The blue eyes of blistering hot summer skies bored into hers with disconcerting and challenging directness. "I also wanted to ask you to dance with me. Will you, Alida?"

Her heart squeezed tight. Gareth Morgan was on the prowl. He *wanted her* again! As easily and as casually as that!

A surge of white-hot rage burned through Alida. Her first inclination was to refuse outright. But then the soul-deep frustration he had dealt her forged into iron purpose.

Gareth Morgan needed to be taught a lesson. He couldn't know it—he would not even conceive such a possibility—but his sins of five years ago were about to come home to roost. She would show him the same blackness of heart he had shown her. Exactly the same! She would be every bit as ruthless in her treatment of him as he had been with her. Let him learn what it felt like!

"Yes," she said, rising slowly to her feet. "Yes, I'll have this one dance with you."

He didn't smile. Perhaps the bitter hardness in her heart was reflected in her eyes. Perhaps he sensed some danger to himself. ''Thank you,'' he said, his eyes narrowing slightly.

Alida had the sharp impression he had anticipated a refusal, which he had determined to fight. Her ready acquiescence had shifted the ground between them. But there was no hint of retreat from him. He meant to go on, no matter what he met.

Alida swept a smile at her friends. ''Please excuse me.''

Her mind didn't register their replies. They were totally irrelevant. Everyone and everything in the ballroom became totally irrelevant as she took the arm Gareth Morgan offered her. The whole world had shrunk to contain only him and herself. Which was precisely how it had felt before. The only difference was that Alida now held control, which Gareth Morgan could not foresee.

''Why did you accept your sister's invitation to come here?'' she asked lightly as they moved towards the dance floor. ''You must have been bored out of your mind.''

''I'd be a most unmannerly bore if I admitted to that,'' he demurred.

She sliced him a look that mocked his smooth side-step.

He made a rueful grimace. ''I said too much five years ago.''

She felt his hold on her arm tighten. ''Yes, I remember it well.'' She tossed the words at him in disdain, as if it didn't matter.

"I'm sorry. Will you accept my apology now?"

"Why apologise? At least you had the decency to speak the truth in the end. I wouldn't change that. However unpalatable it might be, I prefer directness to social niceties."

She felt his eyes on her but she didn't look at him. She kept her face utterly impassive, her gaze fixed on where they were heading.

"Perhaps lies would have been kinder," he suggested, as if musing on that idea for the first time.

"Perhaps." She threw him a fleeting little smile, a nothing smile that he could interpret any way he liked.

"I'm sorry. I should have thought more about you. I recall that at the time I was certainly not feeling kind. I was feeling very direct and—" he paused, his voice dropping to a low murmur "—exceedingly primitive."

He had taken her at her word about being direct and was going straight to the heart of his purpose. Alida took a deep breath. Exceedingly primitive was a good description for what had happened between them. It was also a good description of what she was feeling right now. Revenge. An eye for an eye, a tooth for a tooth.

"You haven't answered my question, Gareth," she reminded him, changing the topic, not letting him see her purpose. "Why are you here?" She couldn't afford to let her feelings show. Not yet.

He released a short sigh. "My sister's husband is in New Zealand. She inveigled me to take his place as her escort. I owe her some indulgence so I came with her," he stated matter-of-factly. Then in a softer, more intimate tone, he added, "But from the moment I knew you would be present, I was not bored, Alida."

"Oh? What did you feel?" she inquired lightly.

"Excitement, vitality, intensely alive, invigorated..."

The throb of promising sexuality in his voice pummelled her heart. He was not pulling any punches, Alida thought grimly. She paused at the edge of the dance floor, digesting the fact that he had not actively sought a chance to see her again, but the thought of her had done something to him. The excitement of the chase, the pursuit, the capture.

There had been no plan to establish any kind of relationship with her. But for his brother-in-law's absence Gareth would not be here at all. He was simply picking up on an opportunity. And going for it flat out. That knowledge cemented her resolve to make him pay for the pain he had given her.

She looked at him with flat, empty eyes. "When did you know I would be present, Gareth?"

"I read your name in this evening's newspaper."

She raised her eyebrows. "Did that evoke interesting memories, or interesting possibilities?" she asked derisively.

"Both." The blue eyes glittered with some indefinable emotion. Resentment? Anger? A bitter acceptance of something he couldn't control? "Is that what you wanted to hear, Alida?"

"How is your wife, Gareth?" she shot back at him. "Still giving you your sexual freedom?"

His face tightened as though she had slapped him. "Kate died six months ago," he said quietly.

The shock of that statement brought a sudden rush of shame for the callous way she had spoken. "I'm sorry."

His eyes mocked her. "Do you really care, Alida?"

That stung her out of her shame. She had nothing to be ashamed of. Nothing! "No," she flung at him, all the blackness in her heart coming to the surface. She wouldn't let him know she cared. All Kate Morgan had meant to her was pain. But it wasn't the poor woman's fault. It was all her own for loving a man she could never possess.

"You don't mince your words." His voice had hardened. Clearly that had stung him, despite his cynicism about her feelings.

"I told you I prefer directness."

"I loved Kate." There was the throb of deep emotion in his voice this time. He knew how to hurt, too.

The wounds of the past were well and truly open now. "You might recall I never got to know her. I'm sorry you lost someone you loved. But I didn't know her," she said fiercely. "You meant nothing to me when I went to Riordan River. And neither did she. I didn't know you were married until you told me about your wife."

His eyes burned into hers, challenging her statement, not believing it. "If my marriage concerns you, why did you accept my invitation to dance, believing my wife was still alive?''

She sensed the same violence of feeling in him that was churning through her. She lifted her chin in scornful defiance of what he thought of her. ''You opened the door to memories, Gareth,'' she flung at him. ''And I wanted to hurt you with them.''

''You're doing a good job of it.''

''You came to me,'' she reminded him. ''I didn't come to you.''

''Then try coming to me now,'' he said bitterly.

He didn't wait for a reply. He swung her into his arms, pulling her close to him as he steered her into the throng of dancing couples, moving with an aggressive sureness of step and total confidence in his power to rekindle the physical attraction that had once before exploded into compelling need.

Alida did not resist. All her defiance and bitter resolutions were caving in under the shattering knowledge that Gareth was not married any more. The feel of his body against her own weakened her even further. She no longer had any clear idea of where this might lead. All she could think of was that Gareth was free.

CHAPTER THREE

THE BAND WAS PLAYING "Hey Jude." The hour was late. The frenetic earlier energy had given way to the more languorous beat of soulful songs.

Gareth held her intimately against his body, ensuring she would have no trouble following his every step. She could feel the hard play of his muscles as he swept her effortlessly around the floor, using the seductive rhythm to turn every movement into a tantalising exercise in sensuality.

He was very good at doing what he was doing, Alida thought. She had given up on her body. It was far too hungry for the feelings he aroused to take any notice of cerebral instructions.

Every slide of his hard muscular thighs against hers sent a quiver of excitement through her stomach. Gareth was over six feet tall, but her own above-average height and the high heels she wore made them well-matched for the subtle sexuality he employed in his dancing. The palm of his hand in the pit of her back pressured the vertebrae of her spine, controlling her movements, their togetherness. It was a pressure that made her extremely aware of his masculinity, of her femininity.

Perhaps it was stupidly defeatist of her to still want him. But she did. No man measured up to Gareth Morgan. Not before or since. He had scarred her life with such careless, arrogant ease, yet somehow that didn't seem to matter now. She loved the touch of him, the feel of him, the scent of him, the thought of him.

Common sense insisted he only wanted to use her again and she should not let him have this effect on her. It was wrong. Hopelessly, hurtfully wrong. His wife's death did not change Gareth's opinion of her. She was not a woman he would ever take seriously. He simply did not see her as a woman he could love. Or want to love. He had loved Kate. Still loved the memory of her. Whereas she . . .

"Alida." The gravelly murmur was a command for her attention.

She looked up reluctantly, hoping that her eyes did not reveal her intense desire for him.

There was a grim set to his face, a dark world of torment in his eyes that told her she had certainly aroused memories that hurt. "If you had known I was married would you have acted differently?" he asked.

Had she made him feel guilty for using her as he had? Did he want his conscience cleared? Or did he simply want to feel justified in what he had done? Once again the primitive urge to revenge herself on him seared her mangled heart. He should pay for his callous treatment of her!

Yet if she was totally honest with herself, could she have resisted him when he started making love to her, when he had already seduced her with his eyes, arousing so much need, promising every answer to it? Would she have thought of Kate Morgan when Gareth himself had filled her mind to the exclusion of everything else?

"No," she answered flatly. "The only difference would have been that afterwards I would have hated you more."

His mouth curled in self-mockery. "If it gives you any satisfaction, I hated myself enough for us both."

"Did you feel guilt enough for both of us, too?" she asked derisively.

She could see the withdrawal in his eyes, the flicker of pain that was too private to share, and she wished she hadn't said that. What good could it do to keep lashing out at him? He was free of his marriage now. If there was any chance of her having a real relationship with Gareth Morgan, she could only destroy it by endlessly reminding him of the wife he had loved.

It was probably crazy to hope there might be any chance at all. Yet if there was, shouldn't she try for it? Not just for herself. She didn't have only herself to consider.

"It went beyond control, Alida," Gareth said quietly. "I don't know why. A mesh of circumstances, the time, the place, you. There's no excuse."

"No. There's no excuse." She heaved a sigh to relieve her pent-up feelings. Before she could stop them, more accusing words spilled from her lips. "If you'd left me alone. Avoided me..."

"How does one avoid the unavoidable? You're the most desirable woman I've ever met." His mouth quirked into a little movement that projected apologetic appeal. "I know that's no excuse."

Was he flattering her or telling the truth? Whichever, this dwelling on the past only served to keep stirring the deep bitterness she harboured. Better to put it aside. She had to think about the future.

She gave him an ironic little smile. "You're a desirable man, Gareth. That's no excuse, either."

She felt his chest rise and fall against her breasts. Hungry need simmered into his eyes. He moved the hand he was holding to his shoulder, released it, then slowly stroked his fingers down the long silky fall of her hair.

"I tried very hard to forget you, Alida. I tried to forget what happened between us."

The thought of him failing to control himself over her, failing to forget what had happened, was like an aphrodisiac, fanning her memories of the wild passion they had known together. "So did I... try to forget," she answered huskily.

His eyes searched hers, feeding off her susceptibility to his words. "I didn't succeed," he said.

"Neither did I," she replied recklessly. Perhaps he wouldn't cut her off so cruelly this time. Perhaps he would learn to care for her.

"You did not seem to be attached to any of the men at your table."

Would it deter him if she was, Alida wondered? If she was prepared to give in to him, would he have any scruples about sweeping any other man aside to take what he wanted? How much did Gareth want her this time? How far would he go?

"I don't have a partner, if that's what you mean," she replied, opening the door for him, telling herself she would act just like Gareth, taking what she wanted. If it led to the kind of relationship she needed with him... But if it didn't, she would use him as he had used her. Why not? She was thirty years old, unmarried, unloved except by her family. And Gareth Morgan was the only man she wanted.

"There is no man in your life at present?"

No man since him, Alida thought in bitter irony. If only he knew. But he would never find that out. It would be admitting too much. She had to know a lot more about the heart and mind of Gareth Morgan, and be sure he was worthy of her confidences, before she could consider revealing all that had resulted from her first encounter with him.

"Not at present," she answered.

His face relaxed. Satisfaction glinted in his eyes. The questioning was over for the time being. He had secured the ground he wanted—everything cleared for him to move in on her. He proceeded to do so.

The hand that had stroked her hair slid to her back, gently pressing her closer. Alida gave in to the temptation to slide her hands around his neck and lean into him. He bent his head. She felt the warmth of his breath waver through her hair. He stroked her back with light knowing fingers, weaving a web of intense sensitivity to his touch.

The dance went on, building the tension between them, teasing the memories of all the primitive intimacies they had once shared with each other. Alida felt the forceful stirring of his manhood, revelled in his inability to repress it, moved her body to incite his desire.

"Alida." It was very close to an animal growl, the heat of his breath tingling on her ear. "We're not playing games. Yes or no."

Her need for him went beyond the purely sexual. She had to try for more. Her self-respect demanded it. "What would I be saying yes to, Gareth? A one-night stand? Is that what you want me for?"

His mouth moved over her hair, and she sensed the yearning in him to sate all his senses with her. "I'm here until Monday. God knows if it will be enough. Maybe I can make some other arrangements. I don't know, Alida. Don't ask me for promises."

Monday. Four nights, three days. Could she make him care enough about her in so little time? What if tonight was all he really wanted? But what alternative did she have? Gareth was right. There was no time to play games, to find out if he was speaking the truth. He wouldn't respect her for that anyway. He would depart as he had done before. And that would be the end.

She dropped all thought of revenge. An eye for an eye and a tooth for a tooth wasn't all that much comfort when you were lonely. Her heart quivered between hope and despair as she gave him the answer he wanted.

"I want you, Gareth."

He stopped dancing. His hand slid under her hair to the nape of her neck, curling around it, tilting her head back. His piercing blue eyes blazed into hers, turbulent green pools of intense vulnerability and despair.

"We're both mad. You know that. It can't lead anywhere that will satisfy either one of us."

He was warning her that there was no future for them. But there could be, Alida thought feverishly, if only he would allow the possibility.

"You don't have the monopoly on madness, Gareth," she said wryly.

His hand moved to gently stroke her cheek. "Perhaps we're both fools, as well," he said softly. "Always have been."

"Perhaps," she whispered.

"You have a place where we can go?" he asked.

"Yes."

"Now?"

She nodded.

"Then let's go."

His arm went around her shoulders, holding her close to his side. They headed towards her table. Alida was grateful for the physical support. Her legs felt weak and shaky.

''What about your sister?'' she asked.

''She has the chauffeur to take her home. I told her I would make my own way to her place,'' he answered.

Alida's eyes flew to his in sharp inquiry. Had he been so certain of getting his way with her? God! He was so arrogantly self-assured, manipulating everything to suit his needs!

He gave her a twisted little smile. ''If you'd refused me I would have headed for the nearest bar to drown my sorrows.''

''So the choice was between me and the bar,'' she observed dryly.

''The bar was definitely a very second preference.''

''And your sister obliged,'' she said even more dryly, remembering her earlier thoughts on the obliging nature of his sister.

''We had a rather sharp argument on our way here tonight. I didn't feel like having another tête-à-tête with her on the trip home. I guess she felt the same way.''

''What did you argue about?''

He shrugged dismissively. ''Various things.''

''Such as?''

''They're not important now.''

His eyes told her that wanting to be with her, having her, was the only important thing. Alida would have liked to know what he had argued about with his sister. She wanted to know everything he cared about, everything he thought, everything he felt. If only he would let her into his life!

At least tonight might give her some sort of a foothold. His wife was no longer a barrier. Perhaps Gareth wanted her for more than to satisfy his transient desire. If she pleased him enough, perhaps there was a chance. Yet the greatest likelihood was that she was making a total fool of herself again. Well, if she was, she would be a fool in her own individual way.

She looked ahead to her table. What were her friends going to think? What were Deborah Hargreaves and the rest of her party going to think? She shook her head. It didn't matter what they thought. She was doing what was right for her.

She glanced at the faces of her friends surreptitiously watching her approach, Jill's expression wary, Suzanne's fascinated, Ivan's speculative. Alida wondered what they read on her face, what they read on Gareth's. Was it plain to see that they were about to go to bed together? She hoped not.

There was little justification for that hope. After all, it was the commonly held view that the fashion set had no compunctions or morals about doing such things. By admitting her susceptibility to his attraction, she hadn't even cleared Gareth's mind of that opinion.

Her friends smiled at her as she reached her chair. Alida managed a responding smile. "If you'll excuse me, Gareth has offered to take me home," she announced.

"A fitting end to a brilliant night," Ivan rolled out, his bright brown eyes twinkling delight.

"Don't forget the statuette!" Suzanne cried, reaching out for it to hand it over.

Jill forestalled her, picking it up and presenting it to Alida with a flourish. "Alida, you have done us all proud," she said warmly.

"We did it together," Alida replied.

Gareth picked up her handbag and bade her friends good night. They chorused something back. She didn't really hear. Gareth's hand was on her arm, drawing her away. Then he was steering her towards the exit from the ballroom.

This could very well be the most important night of my life, Alida thought, then glanced in wry whimsy at the statuette in her hand. It meant absolutely nothing compared to what Gareth Morgan could mean to her. Once again he had changed everything for her. She desperately hoped it would be for the better this time. Not only for her sake . . . but also for the son Gareth didn't know he had.

CHAPTER FOUR

THE TAXI PULLED AWAY from the hotel. It was at least a twenty-minute trip to Claremont, where Alida lived. She was grateful for that fact. It gave her time to examine what she was doing. It also gave her time to change her mind if she wanted to.

Then Gareth reached across and took her hand in his, strong fingers curling around hers, stroking them as though savouring the soft texture of her skin. Holding hands seemed oddly juvenile, yet there was nothing juvenile about what Gareth's touch did to her. He might have been clutching her heart, making it pump faster, spreading an aching need through her entire body.

She glanced at him and found him studying her, as though absorbing every detail. He gave her a half smile that held appreciation. It was perfectly plain he was not harbouring doubts about what he wanted or his course of action.

"What are you doing in Perth, Gareth?" she asked.

He shrugged. "I have some business to transact." He hesitated, frowned, then reluctantly added, "I wanted to spend some time with my daughter, as well."

"I didn't know that." The words spilled out.

He looked at her oddly.

"That you had a daughter," Alida explained, hoping that she didn't look and sound as stricken as she felt. The idea of Gareth having a child—children?—from his marriage had never crossed her mind. None had been in evidence when she had been at Riordan River. But then his wife had not been there, either.

He winced at her surprise. "I did have some normal years of marriage, Alida."

A painful flush washed up her neck and burned into her cheeks. "Yes, of course," she mumbled and snapped her head away, looking blindly out the side window. How would he feel about having another child, one who had not been born to his beloved wife? How would his daughter feel about a half brother born from adultery?

"Do you have any other children?" she asked, trying to keep all emotion out of her voice.

"No."

"How old is she?"

He expelled a breath as though impatient with this line of conversation. "Stacey is thirteen. She started at boarding school this year. She's not settling very well. She misses—well, she misses me and the life she's known up until now."

And her mother, Alida added for him. A girl would always miss her mother. Especially at thirteen when her life was changing in so many ways. Alida well remembered her own problems when she had been sent away to school. Gareth's daughter would undoubtedly have a lot of adjusting to do.

Would she ever accept another woman in her mother's place? But that was leaping too far ahead, Alida reminded herself. First things first. If Gareth was only after satisfaction with her, there was little point in worrying over a future.

Unless he could come to love her.

Yes, that was what she really wanted, Alida acknowledged. For Gareth to return the love he had left stillborn in her five years ago. Despite the way he had treated her then, he could still stir the same feelings that yearned for fulfilment.

Could she live with less, she wondered? Was she willing to compromise if it meant Andy would have his father? If it meant she could have Gareth as a constant in her life, even if it was only a part-time constant? Was there any real chance of having something good with him that would not cost her her self-respect?

Alida slowly regained her composure. She turned to look at the man who could mean so much to her and her son. His gaze was fixed on the road ahead, but not seeing it. Alida's heart sank. By speaking of his daughter, she had obviously reminded him of his wife again.

She saw his mouth compress into a thin line. Then his hand tightened around hers and he swung his head towards her, blue eyes glittering. When he found her looking at him, his expression softened.

"Tell me what you've been doing over the past five years," he invited.

"Working." Her smile mocked any further pursuit of that topic. "I don't want to bore you, Gareth."

He glanced at the statuette on the seat between them. "You obviously worked to good effect. I don't imagine that such an award comes easily."

"It was a goal to aim for."

"And you reached it." He lifted his gaze and searched her eyes, curious to see what she felt about it.

"Yes."

"Have you now achieved your life's ambition?"

"No. I have other goals." He could misinterpret that statement as much as he liked. She was not going to elaborate to him on the way her mind was working.

His mouth curled into a sardonic smile. "To reach the top of any field, you have to dedicate your life to it, Alida. Is there room for anything else apart from your ambition?"

"I'm making room for you, Gareth," she answered bluntly.

"Tonight you are."

"Yes. For tonight." To see if it was a beginning or a dead end, she thought.

His fingers dragged back and forth over hers, transmitting the tension that held them both captive to the unanswered questions that throbbed between them.

"How old are you?" he asked quietly.

"Thirty."

"You haven't wanted to marry?"

She knew he had her pigeonholed as a woman whose career came first and foremost. "It hasn't happened."

"Does your career get in the way?"

"No."

He frowned. "Then why?"

"I loved a man once. It takes two people to marry, Gareth."

"Who was he?"

"No one I could introduce you to," she said evasively.

"I'm sorry," he said sympathetically, totally unaware that she had been speaking of him.

"Are you?" Alida tossed at him. "We wouldn't be in this taxi if I was committed to someone else, Gareth."

His mouth twisted. "You mean you wouldn't do what I did?"

"Precisely."

"It wouldn't have stopped me from wanting you, Alida."

She shrugged. "I don't really care about desire."

There was a raw yearning in his eyes that choked the breath in her throat. *His* marriage hadn't stopped him from taking what he wanted last time. Would *her* hypothetical marriage have held him back from approaching her again? How ruthless was Gareth in going after what he wanted? How much did he want her? He had once been contemptuous of her supposedly loose standards of morality. What were his standards?

"If you don't care about desire, Alida, why am I with you?" he asked, a hard note of suspicion in his voice.

Had he leapt to the thought that she might have played him along to wreak the kind of revenge she had initially had in mind? "Perhaps I didn't want to be by myself," she answered.

He probed her eyes for long tense moments before relaxing with a rueful sigh. "In the loneliness of the night," he half mused. "I guess we all know how that feels. The problem is in how much lonelier you feel afterwards."

The comment gave Alida the opportunity to ascertain where she stood with him. "Was I one of many that you had because of..."

"No." He gave a harsh derisive laugh. "Believe it or not, I found celibacy easier to live with than guilt. There was only you, Alida."

The jolt to her heart was instant. She shook her head in stunned disbelief. "Are you saying that except for me you stayed faithful to your wife all through your marriage?"

"Is that so surprising?" he mocked, then cynically added, "yes, I suppose it is in the fast lane where you live."

"Fidelity is not exclusive to your set of people, Gareth," she retorted sharply, hating his false assumption about her but knowing she had no means of correcting it. "You must have loved Kate very much."

A strange conflict played across his face as though he was no longer sure of what he felt for the woman he had married. "Kate was my wife," he said. To him that was obviously explanation enough for the way he had stood by her.

Alida felt painfully confused. All her preconceptions about Gareth were crashing around her. "Why me?" she asked huskily. "Why choose me?"

"Does one *choose* mutual attraction? Did you *choose* me, Alida?"

He was right. Choice hadn't come into it. It was like a fever in the blood that had caught both of them unprepared for what would follow.

But she had been the only one, Alida thought on a rising wave of hope. No other woman had stirred him as she had. Surely that meant there was a chance for this strong attraction to grow into something deeper now there was no reason to stunt it or cut it dead.

On the other hand, Gareth hadn't come looking for her. He still didn't *choose* her. None of his prejudices about the sort of woman she was had been wiped out, and Alida knew that words wouldn't achieve that end. He had to see, to learn for himself. Could that be done in four nights and three days?

The challenge of desire burned in his eyes, forcing an acknowledgment that she shared it with him, inciting the response that only he had ever drawn from her. It was impossible to control the instinctive chemistry stirring into urgent life inside her, suffusing her limbs with a sweet heavy ache, exciting fluttery little tremors through her stomach, bringing a tingle of sensitivity to her breasts. She wasn't even aware of the taxi slowing to a halt outside her house.

"This is it, isn't it?" the driver inquired when neither Gareth nor Alida moved.

Alida confirmed that they had arrived at the right destination. Gareth paid the fare, then helped her out of the car.

"Your house?" Gareth asked, a note of surprise in his voice as he scanned its conventional facade. It was not a luxurious house, by any means, more a good solid brick home with no outstanding features except for the artistic landscaping of the garden.

"Yes," Alida answered briefly. Gareth's arm was around her waist, his hand resting on her hip. The warmth of his palm seemed to burn through her silk culotte. She was vibrantly aware of his body brushing against hers as they walked up the front path.

"Wouldn't an apartment suit you better?" he asked curiously.

"I prefer my own space."

And space for Andy to play outdoors, she added silently. It was fortunate her darling little boy was out of the way at the moment. It wouldn't do to let Gareth see him until such time as it might prove right. She would telephone her parents tomorrow, tell them she was delayed in Perth for a few more days. Andy wouldn't mind. He loved being with his grandparents and uncles. Life at the Rose homestead was far more fascinating than the enforced boundaries of a house in suburban Perth.

With a heart-sickening jolt, Alida suddenly remembered the bathroom. Andy's play toys were lined along the bathtub ledge. She would have to hide them. Her mind swept through the rest of the house, trying to recollect if there were other things of Andy's lying around in full view. She couldn't think of any. Gareth would have no occasion to look into Andy's bedroom. The only bedroom that concerned him was hers.

Her heart beat faster as she unlocked the front door and pushed it open. Her legs were trembling as she stepped forward into the hallway. She switched on the overhead light and moved to the console table where she set down the statuette and her handbag. The door clicked shut behind her. She took a deep breath in a vain attempt to calm her shrieking nerves, then swung around to face Gareth.

"Would you like a cup of coffee?" she asked with brittle brightness.

"No." It was little more than a breath from his lips. His eyes told her unmistakably what he wanted. The frank explicit message was both frightening and enthralling. His skin looked tightly stretched across the strong bone structure of his face, and she shivered in anticipation, recognising the taut waiting hunger that had once been unleashed with barbaric passion.

Gareth's thin veneer of civilisation was disappearing before her eyes. There was strength and authority in the hand that took hers and pulled her against his body, uncompromising purpose in the arm that slid around her waist to hold her there. The adrenaline pumping through her bloodstream made Alida feel light-headed. She wanted his mouth to come down on hers, wanted the kisses that would shut out the rest of the world. Only a persistent beat of sanity cried a warning against it.

Remember afterwards, it said. Remember how he turned away from you when his passion had all been spent. He didn't care about you, and he still doesn't. If you let him use you as he did before, it will be the same, wife or no wife. He will consume all you give him, and you'll be left with ashes again.

A shudder of pain ran through her as he bent his head towards her. "No! Don't!" she choked out, and wrenched her head aside.

She felt Gareth's body stiffen, heard a terse impatience in his voice. "What's the matter?"

"I...I can't do this, Gareth. Let me go. Please," she begged, her hands kneading his chest in agitation while the rest of her body churned in upheaval at the denial she was forcing upon it.

She wanted him so desperately. He was so close. Everything within her yearned for the fulfilment he promised. But it was a false promise. Everything he had said, the way he had acted—he only wanted to take, not give.

A hand grasped her chin, turned her face to his. The blue eyes blazed with angry questions. "Why?" he demanded.

"Because..." *Because I love you. I always have, fool that I am. But you don't love me, Gareth Morgan, and you're going to break my heart into little jagged pieces again, and leave me in a far worse state of desolation than you did before, and I can't bear it.* A huge lump swelled into her throat and tears welled in her eyes.

"Alida?" His brows lowered in puzzlement. The arm around her relaxed its hold. The hand on her chin moved to gently cup her cheek.

"I'm sorry," she blurted out. "I'm not playing games. I meant to—"

"Tell me what's wrong," he commanded urgently.

"You are. About so many things. I thought I could use you as you want to use me, but I'm not like that, Gareth. I'm not. And it's no use thinking I can be. I just can't take being used again."

"Alida." It was a rasp of protest. His hands moved to her upper arms, rubbing them in a soothing way. Then he heaved a ragged sigh and stepped back from her, his face tight with frustration, his eyes sick with it, confused and accusing.

Alida felt sick, too. Tears spilled down her cheeks in a miserable dribble as she stared at the man she had loved and hated and wanted for so long. Why couldn't it be different? Why couldn't he have courted her decently, as he must have courted his wife? Why did he judge her so meanly?

He lifted his hand in a stiff, awkward gesture of offering. "Is there anything I can do?" he asked.

"For a woman who lives in the fast lane?" she choked out bitterly. "You don't care about how I feel, Gareth. You never did. Your desire is only to take."

Her legs felt as though they were flowing with heavy treacle, boneless. Somehow she forced them to move, to support her as she turned and stepped to the console table. "I'll ring for a taxi. You won't have to wait long," she said, reaching for the telephone.

"Why are you doing this, Alida?"

His voice was low and strained. She paused, yearning for him to be sincerely sympathetic, then shook her head with bleak resignation. "There's nothing for you to stay for, Gareth. I won't change my mind."

"You shared yourself with me once," he reminded her. "Won't you let me give you something in return?"

"Like what?" She swept him with a dull, derisive look.

"Company. You said you didn't want to be by yourself tonight."

"Yes. I said that. But what company would you be, Gareth? All you do is judge me contemptuously. I don't want to hear any more of your prejudices. They hurt." Her eyes raked his with pained accusation, then dropped to the award she had won. She picked up the statuette. "You think this represents ambition."

"Doesn't it?"

A harsh, bitter laugh scraped from her throat. "Have you ever worked hard to keep from thinking of other things, Gareth? To wear yourself out so you'll sleep at night?"

"Yes. I've done that," he answered quietly.

"Are there national awards for good management of a cattle station?"

"Not that I know of."

"But you give yourself goals."

"Yes."

"Well, so did I. So did I," she repeated sadly as she set the statuette on the table again. "Years of hard work to stave off the loneliness—that's what this award represents to me, Gareth. And you know what I felt when I went up on stage to get it tonight?"

"Tell me."

"I didn't feel anything." She turned to him with a wobbly little smile. "I should have felt something, shouldn't I? It wasn't right to feel nothing."

"You looked proud."

"Yes. And I smiled. I smiled very brightly, like a winner. Except I'm a loser in life, Gareth. The right things don't happen to me. Not the things that I really care about."

"What do you want?"

She stared at him, seeing the restraint he was rigidly applying to keep this conversation calm and reasonable. His hands were clenched at his sides, belying the quiet, soothing words he spoke to her. He was wound tightly like a clock, exerting control by sheer willpower.

The strain showed on his face, making it look older somehow. She saw that the lines carved from nose to mouth were deeper than she remembered. Fine crow's-feet marked the outer corners of his eyes. A few threads of grey glinted in the midnight-black hair. Time moves on and stamps its passage on all of us, she thought. We're both five years older, the circumstances are different, yet everything remains the same between us.

"You wouldn't think of introducing your daughter to me, would you, Gareth? You'd keep her as separate from me as you once kept your wife."

A muscle in his cheek contracted. "I didn't think that far ahead, Alida."

Her mouth twisted. "I know. I'm not a real person to you, am I? You made me up in your head, fashioning an image that suited you, that you could discard as unimportant after I'd served your needs. That way you didn't have to think of me as a person who bleeds inside. People in the fast lane are too busy to bleed, aren't they? And they don't stop to care about children."

He said nothing. But his eyes acknowledged the hit she had made. It gave her no pleasure to see the recoil in them. The truth was too painful.

"I'm sorry, Gareth," she said wearily. "Despite our mutual desires, despite what I said, the sheer naked compulsion of the moment, I'm not going to be a convenience for you whenever opportunity arises. It's too demeaning."

"You're right." He dragged the words out reluctantly. "I'm sorry for misunderstanding, Alida. I'm not good company for you. I see that now. And I'm sorry about that, too. I guess—" his mouth twisted into a grimace of displeasure "—I've been totally selfish where you're concerned. Not thinking of your feelings at all, except in so far as I thought they matched mine."

She said nothing. It was another painful truth.

He inhaled a deep breath and released it in a long slow sigh. His eyes swept over her, as though imprinting this image of her on his mind. "I guess I could do with a long walk," he said softly.

"I'll ring for a taxi," she offered.

He shook his head. "I'd rather walk."

He left without bidding her good-night. Or goodbye.

For a long time Alida stood staring at the door that was shut between them. No hope, she kept telling herself. There never had been any hope. She could have told him about Andy, she supposed, but that would have divided them more. Gareth might have tried to take his son away from her. Or claimed visiting rights. It would have been totally divisive. And there was Andy to consider, as well. Impossible to know how he would have reacted.

No, she had done the right thing. It was easier on everyone if she and Gareth kept apart. If she was unfit to be considered as a possible partner in his life, he would probably think she was unfit to be the mother of his son.

Andy was hers. All hers. Gareth had his daughter, who was all his. That was how it was. That was how it would stay. This feeling of death—it would pass. Everything passed in time.

CHAPTER FIVE

THE NIGHT WAS BRIGHT with stars but Gareth didn't see them. He felt numb and frustrated and bloody wounded. Why was Alida like that? Why had she done that to him?

It was a long walk from Claremont to Peppermint Grove where his sister lived. If the distance made it a punishment for him, so much the better, Gareth thought savagely. He needed some sort of outlet for all the pent-up energy pounding through him, some sort of punishing physical activity to relieve the burning frustrations of his body.

Damn Alida Rose, he thought. Damn the impulse that had made him approach her. Damn the desire that gave rise to the impulse. Hadn't he felt enough guilt over her? He certainly didn't need another load of it!

Yet every word she had said about him was true. He couldn't deny it. Not any of it. She had held up a mirror to him and shown him an image of himself that stripped him of all pretensions to being the human he thought he was. Shame burrowed through his heart as he remembered every callous detail of how he had treated her.

Tonight was bad enough. He had chased her like a stag on the scent, blind to everything but having her again, determined to sweep aside any obstacle to satisfying *his* desire. Over and over again she had signalled the hurt he had given her five years ago, but that hadn't stopped him. He had kept right on, pursuing his purpose, forcing the response he wanted from her.

That bleak wounded look through the tears in her eyes... How many men had hurt her, taking their pleasure of her and leaving her with nothing? Worse than nothing. The humiliation of knowing she had been used only for their gratification. And however many men there had been, *he* was one of them. There was no escaping that fact. *He* had hurt Alida Rose, and he had hurt her badly.

All these years his conscience hadn't been troubled by her. His infidelity to Kate, that had troubled him because of the promise he had made to his wife. Apart from the one occasion with Alida Rose, he had kept that promise. But keeping that promise had exacted a terrible toll. He had dismissed any feelings Alida might have had. His only concern had been the feelings she had given him.

He remembered that after he had taken her, she had asked when she would see him again, expecting what they had shared to go on. He winced at the answer he had given, was compelled to give. It hadn't been easy for him. It must have been harder for her.

He had cut dead the idea of seeing her again, not caring if such a brutal action had made her bleed inside. Knowing the type of world to which she belonged, he hadn't imagined it would cost her very much. All the hurt was on his side. After all, in his mind, she had known from the start that he was married.

But she hadn't known. He had to accept that now. It must have shocked her, shattered her, blown any hopes she had nursed to smithereens. He recalled that she hadn't said a word. Not a single word. He had been relieved when she had silently accepted his situation with Kate. She had left him without trying to reopen the issue.

He had interpreted that action as pragmatic worldliness—the affair was dead—just another experience to chalk up in the life he had coloured for her in his mind. The life he knew nothing about at all in real terms.

The pain in her eyes tonight, the loneliness, there had been nothing he could do to assuage either. He, who had contributed so much to both without a thought for her. No wonder she had wanted him to go. She had every justification not to want his company. Yet he hated the thought of her remembering him like that in the lonely darkness of the night. He wished . . .

His mouth curled in self-derision. Comforting her had nothing to do with what he wanted from holding her in his arms. The desire she aroused in him was still a throbbing ache. He wanted what they'd shared before. He wanted that so much it would probably haunt him to his dying day.

The fair thing to do was stay away from her. He couldn't make up for what he'd done, and he couldn't offer her the kind of relationship she needed. At least he could have the decency to keep right out of her life. If that was what she wanted. But damn it! She had wanted him, too. The mutual attraction was still there, the same as before. Couldn't they share something together? Why deny some mutual pleasure?

Gareth had no idea what hour it was when he finally arrived at his sister's home. He was weary in both body and soul, but when he shed his clothes and dropped into bed, the merciful oblivion of sleep was long in coming. He was tormented by frustrations that were beyond his willpower to control.

He had been so close to having Alida again, the touch of her, the feel of her, the whole softly scented reality of her. His body stirred at the memory, demanding a resolution.

Damn the consequences, he thought. *I want her. And I'm going to have her. I don't know what I'm going to do, or how I'm going to do it, but there is unfinished business between Alida Rose and me. And if I'm half the man I think I am, I'm going to end it my way.*

Eventually he drifted into an uneasy semiconsciousness where dreams of Alida Rose taunting him with the fashion award kept drifting through his mind.

The grey light of dawn was filtering into his room before he fell into deep sleep.

He was stirred from it by an unceremonious shaking and the insistent voice of his daughter. "Come on, Dad! You've got to wake up. It's almost time for me to go to school and I need to know about last night."

He forced open one bleary eye. "What about last night?" he growled.

Stacey plonked herself on the bed beside him and thrust the front page of the morning newspaper in his face. It seemed to be dominated by a photograph of Alida Rose holding up the statuette. It was like a figment of his nightmares. Then he remembered the pose from the presentation ceremony.

"Alida Rose takes top fashion award," Stacey read out aloud.

"So?" he mumbled.

"So Aunty Deb says you danced with her. And took her home afterwards," Stacey informed him in a tone of very eager interest. "What happened? What did you do with her, Dad?"

Gareth silently cursed his sister. She was getting to be an extremely pesky blabbermouth.

"We talked."

"Is that all?"

"Yes," Gareth replied irritably.

"She's very beautiful, isn't she?" Stacey prompted.

"Not bad," he mumbled non-committally.

"You must like her."

"Mmm."

"She must like you, too."

"What is this? A Spanish inquisition?" he protested tersely.

"I guess you got home very, very late, did you, Dad?" Stacey said understandingly. Hopefully?

"Not too late."

"It's all right, Dad," Stacey assured him. "I won't tell Aunty Deb."

"Aunty Deb doesn't know a damned thing!" he snapped, then dragged himself up on one elbow to glower at his daughter whose face was alight with avid curiosity and speculation. "Are you ready for school?"

"No."

"Then get ready."

"I'm almost ready."

"Completely ready."

"Okay." She heaved a resigned sigh and hitched herself off his bed. "I just wanted to know if I didn't have to worry about you any more."

"Worry?"

"You know, about your natural urges being dried up. And drinking too much."

"Stacey." He expelled an impatient and somewhat threatening breath.

"Okay, okay, I'm going." She folded the newspaper and tucked it under her arm. "You don't have to get up, Dad. Aunty Deb said she'd drive me to school. So you can go back to sleep now." There was a smug smile on her face as she headed for the door.

Gareth grimaced at his daughter's retreating back. She was getting to be positively precocious, what with his stupid sister saying things she shouldn't, and a gaggle of silly schoolgirls filling her head with fantasies. On the other hand, at least she didn't seem offended by the idea of Alida Rose.

And then the thought popped into his head. Something Alida had said last night. He had no idea whether it would work or not, but as a scheme it didn't look too bad.

He relaxed on the pillows again, his mind swiftly darting through today's schedule, replanning his time. Did Alida have offices somewhere or did she work from that house? He would have to find out. In fact, he needed to find out all he could about her, get himself informed instead of making ignorant assumptions. This next approach had to be carefully plotted.

His body stirred again at the thought of her. Going back to sleep seemed highly improbable so Gareth threw off the bedclothes and headed for the shower. One thing was certain. *He* didn't have to worry about his natural urges being dried up. At the present moment they needed dampening down. But he wasn't about to tell his daughter that! Nor his blabbermouth sister!

By the time Gareth went down to breakfast—washed, shaved and dressed for the day ahead of him—Deborah had already returned from taking Stacey and her own children to school. She was seated at the table, drinking her umpteenth cup of coffee and doing the daily cryptic crossword, to which she was addicted. As he entered the room, she looked up and bestowed a delighted smile on him.

"Ah, Gareth, just the person to tell me. What's that special breed of cow in Africa that sort of rhymes with bull?"

"Tuli."

"Of course! An African cow with an afterthought. Tulips. That does it," she declared triumphantly.

"What's the afterthought?"

"P.S. As in a letter. Tuli and P.S. equals tulips."

Gareth poured himself a cup of coffee from the simmering percolator and sat down to drink it. He regarded his sister with considerable impatience as she went blithely on with her crossword. Deborah was younger by four years, and most of the time he thought her reasonably sensible, but there were times when he felt like throttling her.

She looked up and grinned at him. "Well, you must be feeling good this morning."

She had the same blue eyes as he, and they were dancing with gleeful knowingness. Her features were similar to his, as well, but softer, more feminine. In actual fact, she was a striking-looking woman with her long black hair and tall figure. Max certainly considered his wife the most beautiful woman in the world, but Max was besotted with her. She had given him two fine sons who were doing very well at primary school, and she was a superb hostess, among other things. She was also an interfering busybody!

"Must I?" Gareth challenged tersely.

Deborah's finely arched eyebrows arched higher. "A bit short of sleep?"

Gareth gritted his teeth. "Deborah, please do me a favour and do not even refer to last night."

Her eyebrows lowered into a frown. Then, hesitantly, "It didn't work out so good?"

"Backward SID with a flower."

Her cryptic-crossword mind worked that out in a fraction of a second. "Disaster?"

"Precisely."

"Oh!" She looked vexed. "I guess I shouldn't have said anything to Stacey."

He gave her a stern look. "No. You shouldn't have."

Deborah shrugged. "Well, I just thought it would be a good idea to prepare her."

"For what?"

"Girls of that age can get very jealous of their fathers. I've been trying to ease Stacey into the idea that she can't expect you to be alone and miserable for the rest of your life."

"I am not miserable, Deborah," he bit out with glowering emphasis. "I've never been miserable."

She cast him a sceptical look. "Do you feel up to some breakfast now?"

"I'll get some in the city." He didn't have time to eat if he was to get through his business before the lunch hour.

Deborah returned to her crossword while Gareth finished his coffee. When he stood up to leave she lifted a bright smiling face.

"Max will be home this evening."

"I'll look forward to seeing him."

"You remember we're giving a dinner party tomorrow night?"

"I haven't forgotten."

"I always think neutral ground is best after a disaster. If you'd like to invite Alida Rose . . ."

"Deborah." He heaved an exasperated sigh. "I can manage my own personal life. By myself. Please indulge me with that liberty. Thank you."

She screwed up her nose at him.

He threw her a quelling look and left, feeling darkly frustrated with his sister's irrepressible nature. She probably meant well, he conceded dubiously, but he still wished she would mind her own business. Her and her high-society dinner parties! If his plan worked today, he certainly didn't want to share Alida with a whole lot of other people.

Gareth Morgan walked out of his sister's house with a purposeful step. The far horizons gleamed in his blue eyes. The determination to beat all adversity was carved on his face.

CHAPTER SIX

JILL PUT ALIDA THROUGH a hectic morning. There were two interviews at the local television channel—one for the daily women's hour program, one for tonight's current affairs show. As Jill said, Alida Rose was hot at the moment, and if she didn't capitalise on that, they'd both be absolute fools.

Personal publicity was always a strain for Alida. Yet in a way she was grateful for the distraction. She didn't want to think about Gareth. That would only bring on the black void of pain he had left her with last night.

"Let's splash out and treat ourselves to a disgustingly expensive lunch," Jill suggested as they left the television studios.

Alida's stomach recoiled from the idea. "I'd rather not today, Jill." She offered a rueful smile. "You know interviews churn me up. One day next week, I promise."

"Okay. Sandwiches in my office then. I want your decision on which clothes are to be photographed for the magazine spreads." She grinned. "I was on the phone to Suzanne at the factory. She says it's a madhouse. Orders are pouring in. Everyone wants to top up their stock of Alida Rose."

"Perhaps I should go there and help," Alida suggested. Anything to keep busy. "You can decide on the photographs, Jill."

"Oh, no, you don't!" Jill gave her a stern look. "I've got you today. Suzanne can handle the orders. Besides, who knows what offers have come into the office since we've been out? I need you at my side, Alida."

"If you say so," Alida meekly agreed, not really caring what she did as long as she was doing something.

Jill used her car phone to check on calls and to order sandwiches from her favourite delicatessen.

Alida reflected that it was Jill who had "discovered" her, not the other way around. Jill Masters picked her own clients and she prided herself on having a stable of stars, or stars in the making. She was very good at what she did. Alida had never regretted accepting her offer, her advice, her sense of direction or her friendship. The only wrong move she had ever made on Alida's behalf was the visit to Riordan River. But that was only in a personal sense. Careerwise it had been a brilliant success.

When they arrived at Jill's office, the receptionist's desk was dominated by a vase of beautifully arranged yellow roses. The woman smiled at Alida. "They're for you, Alida. Mr Poletti sent them." She handed over the accompanying card.

It read. "To my golden girl. Your devoted admirer—Ivan."

For some foolish reason, tears pricked Alida's eyes. Ivan was being his usual flamboyant self, yet . . . Had he seen her need last night? The need that Gareth might have fulfilled. Stupid to ever underestimate Ivan's perception of people. He was uncannily accurate. He was also her friend and he wished her well. Alida took a deep breath and blinked back the moisture in her eyes. At least she had friends. Good friends.

She should call him to thank him, but she didn't feel up to fielding questions on Gareth. Not yet. She would write Ivan a thank-you note. That would avoid the problem for a little while, anyway.

But Alida soon discovered there was no avoiding the problem when it came to Jill. Once they were seated in her office with cups of coffee and the sandwiches, Jill made no bones about leading into the subject.

"Are you seeing Gareth Morgan again?" she asked point-blank.

Alida's heart lurched, but she did her best to mask her feelings with a deadpan face. "No, I'm not," she replied flatly. "I don't expect to see him *ever* again." That should close the subject . . . she hoped.

It did. They talked of other things while they ate lunch. But Alida was conscious of Jill's shrewd grey eyes noting her lack of appetite and her lack of any joie de vivre now that she was out of the public eye.

However, once they had cleared the desk of the remnants of their lunch, it was briskly down to business. Jill kept a file of all Alida's designs. She produced a thick folder from her filing cabinet and they sorted through the sketches, selecting the clothes that would best serve their purpose of pinpointing Alida's unique talent. They were halfway through the task when the telephone on the desk buzzed. Alida went on sorting as Jill answered the call.

"I'll be right out," she instructed, and was already on her feet as she put the receiver down.

"If it's a client, do you want to use this office?" Alida asked.

"No. You stay here," Jill tossed at her as she headed for the door.

Alida didn't look up when the door opened a couple of minutes later. She had no warning at all when Jill announced, "Gareth Morgan wants to see you, Alida."

Her head snapped up, and before any coherent thought could form in her mind, the shock of Jill's announcement was compounded by the impact of Gareth's physical presence. He had already stepped into the office. It wasn't a matter of whether she would see him or not. He was right in front of her, as overwhelming as ever.

He was dressed in similar clothes to those he had worn when she had first met him five years ago—brown riding boots, fawn moleskins that faithfully outlined his lean hips and long powerful legs, a white open-necked shirt and a brown leather jacket.

His eyes locked onto Alida's before she could raise any defences against the power of his attraction—determined and possessive eyes, with no intention of letting go—and once again she felt the thrill of excitement and anticipation pulsing through her body, as though every cell of her being was leaping with a new vibrant expectant life.

"Alida," Jill slid in quickly. "You needn't stay this afternoon. I'm sure I can work out what's best now." Then she shut the door, leaving the two of them alone.

A flush seared across Alida's cheekbones. Gareth gave her a crooked little smile that acknowledged her discomfort, but he was not about to back away.

"You were not easy to find, Alida," he said as he walked slowly towards the desk. "The manageress of the Alida Rose boutique at Claremont said you worked at home, but you might be at the factory today. Suzanne, at the factory, said you were at the television studio. The studio said you'd left with Jill Masters. I finally struck lucky here."

He hitched himself onto a corner of the desk and smiled at her, a wide, appealing smile that set her heart pumping madly. "I'm glad I found you."

"What do you want from me, Gareth?" Alida croaked, her throat hopelessly dry and her mind totally confused by the trouble he'd gone to in pursuing her.

"I had intended inviting you to lunch with me. Unfortunately time ran out on that plan." He checked his wristwatch. "I have to pick my daughter up from school at three-fifteen, which gives me about ten minutes to persuade you to accompany me." He smiled at her again. "Would meeting a thirteen-year-old girl be too much of a bore for you, Alida?"

Alida could barely swallow her surprise. "You want me to meet your daughter?"

"I want you with me," he asserted, not quite answering her question.

"Is this step one in getting to be good friends with me before you race me off to bed?" she asked, too sceptical of his intentions to take the offer at face value.

"That is the general idea," he conceded without batting an eyelash.

"I suppose I should appreciate your honesty."

"We both know it's not going to go away, Alida. Five years didn't make a damned bit of difference. My choice is to do something about it. Will you come with me or not?"

The piercing blue eyes challenged her to be equally honest. He wanted her and was going all out for what he wanted—whatever it took. Alida struggled with herself. Impossible to deny she wanted him. It would probably come to the same end, but at least he was not excluding her from meeting his daughter. This way there was a slight chance of some positive relationship developing between them.

"I'll come," she said decisively. Her green eyes flashed a hard warning. "But I don't know if this plan of yours is going to work."

He smiled happily. "Neither do I. The first part of the plot, as I understand it, is that we'll probably go to Stacey's favourite hangout and have banana splits. After that I believe a movie is on the schedule. Something called *Look Who's Talking*. I do hope you have the stomach for hamburgers and French fries at McDonald's because I'm afraid that will be the dinner menu. But you can wash it down with a chocolate thick shake.'' He gave her a rueful look of appeal. ''Does that all sound too abominable?''

She eyed him consideringly, privately amazed that he was prepared to share his daughter to this extent. Then hard cold reason insisted that more likely, in his mind, his daughter was totally irrelevant. She was being used as a means to further his purpose in breaking down the resistance he had met last night.

''When you go after something you go full bore, don't you?'' she accused.

''I do what has to be done,'' came the unequivocal reply. ''Don't you, Alida?''

''I don't think I'd ever do things your way, Gareth,'' she said slowly.

''Maybe you'll change your mind about that.'' The challenge of desire simmered in his eyes, making her extremely conscious of the responses he evoked in her body. ''Our ten minutes is up,'' he added abruptly. ''Let's go meet Stacey.''

Alida rose slowly from her chair. Her legs did not feel steady. Gareth watched her, making her extremely conscious of the way her outfit accentuated the womanliness of her figure. The coordinated two-piece was one of her favourite creations, especially chosen for her television appearance, but she doubted Gareth was taking in its artistic detail.

The top was a white cotton-knit pullover featuring embroidered panels that combined the yellow-gold flower spikes of banksia with its fine soft green leaves. The wide rib clung to the curve of waist and hip. Graceful flowing sleeves were caught into embroidered cuffs just below the elbow. The pullover was teamed with a yellow-gold culotte in a cotton-poly fabric that fell neatly into inverted pleats. Flat white sandals, intricately woven into thin straps of leather, and a matching white shoulder bag completed the outfit.

As she rounded the desk, Alida felt Gareth's eyes burning through her clothes, making her skin prickle with sensitivity. When she swung around to face him, she found him totally still, as though intensely absorbed in the picture he was forming of her in his mind.

"I'm ready," she said curtly.

His gaze flicked up the long silky fall of her caramel-butter hair and fastened on the deep green pools of her eyes. His smile tripped her heart into hammering wildly.

"Ivan is right. A golden girl. But not his, I trust," he observed sardonically as he slid off the desk.

She laughed, more out of nervous relief than amusement. "Hardly. I'm not his type. Ivan is of a different persuasion to you, Gareth. And you shouldn't read other people's letters."

"The card was on open view. On the receptionist's desk," he excused, strolling over to the door for her. "Why is he your devoted admirer?"

"It's a matter of pleasing his artistic eye," she retorted dryly. "He sells my fabric designs."

"Ah! Business."

The dismissive way he said that stung Alida. When he opened the door and gestured her to walk ahead of him she deliberately paused beside him, fixing him with a cool challenging look. "Ivan Poletti is also my very good friend. Loyal, caring and supportive. Try beating that, Gareth."

Then she swept past him and led the way out, waving a farewell salute to a smug-looking Jill and her highly interested receptionist. Gareth caught up with her at the elevator. He said not a word until they were in the small compartment, heading down to the ground floor.

"I can give you what he can't," he said to her.

She met his eyes. "You overrate that, Gareth," she said dismissively.

"No, I don't."

"Yes, you do."

"You only live once, Alida."

The elevator doors opened onto the foyer of the office building. Gareth took her arm to steer her to wherever they were going. His closeness, the warmth of his hand, the words he had spoken . . . all clouded her mind, tantalising her with the idea of succumbing to the needs he aroused. It would be so easy to give in and take what satisfaction she could from being with him, however temporarily.

But she was playing for higher stakes here. She had to keep remembering that. She wondered how much Gareth would give in to her if she kept holding him off. Would he have chased after her today if she had shared her bed with him last night? Would he have asked her to meet his daughter if he had already got what he wanted? How far would he go to satisfy *his* need for her?

It was an interesting question, and Alida pondered it as Gareth escorted her to a white Mercedes. "My sister's car," he muttered dismissively as he opened the passenger door.

"Not your style?" Alida mocked.

He shrugged. "For getting around the city, it's fine."

It meant nothing to him as a status symbol, Alida thought. Gareth Morgan would always scorn status symbols as totally meaningless. He was complete unto himself—except for his present aggravating desire for her. Which he wanted to dispense with at the earliest opportunity.

She waited until they were both settled in the car before asking, "What school does your daughter attend?"

He slanted her a half smile. "Stacey... her name is Stacey. And she's at Heatherton."

It was the most expensive private school in Perth. And the snobbiest, Alida recollected, if it was still the same as when she had attended one of the cheapest boarding schools. She supposed Deborah Hargreaves would have recommended it to her brother.

"Is Stacey expecting to meet me?"

He hesitated. "Not exactly expecting." He cocked an eyebrow at her. "How could she when I wasn't sure what to expect myself? But she knows we were together last night."

That surprised Alida. "You talked about me?"

"Briefly."

"What did she think?"

He cast her a simmering look. "She thinks you're very beautiful."

The compliment brought a flush of pleasure before Alida thought to question, "How does she have any idea?"

"From the photograph in this morning's newspaper."

Perhaps the award had been worth winning after all, Alida thought, if it meant winning a ready approval from Gareth's daughter. If the girl was disposed to like her, Alida was more than willing to meet her halfway. Hope blossomed anew. With Stacey on her side, Gareth might come to view the situation differently. A girl of Stacey's age was in need of a woman's guidance and sympathy.

As they drove through the impressively pillared gateway to Heatherton, it was obvious that the girls had already been released from their last lessons of the day. They were streaming down the paths leading from the classroom block to the various boarding houses in the beautifully kept grounds.

Manicured lawns, rose gardens, tennis courts, hockey fields, old brick buildings dressed with ivy... Heatherton lived and breathed old money, and a great deal of it. Perhaps it was easy to ignore status symbols when you've belonged to old money for generations, Alida mused. Perhaps you simply took them for granted.

Gareth Morgan and his daughter were of that class. One of the great landowning families, established as such since the territory was opened up for settlement. It was not surprising that Gareth considered her business trivial, but she wished he wasn't quite so dismissive of it. Her work was worth more respect than he gave it. Gareth's lack of respect for it reflected on her personally, and she didn't want that to rub off on his daughter.

"Just in time," Gareth muttered, swinging the Mercedes into a parking bay in the visitors' area. He swiftly alighted and strode around the car to Alida's side.

She felt a flutter of nerves as he opened the door for her. "Stacey won't know which car I'm using so it's better if we get out," Gareth explained. "Easier for her to spot us."

Alida had no sooner joined Gareth than a couple of high-pitched squeals drew their attention. A huddle of young schoolgirls stared at them from the nearest path, their eyes agog, their mouths moving in busy whispers to each other. Two broke away from the group and scuttled up the path while the others remained staring at Alida.

"I think you have been recognised," Gareth observed dryly.

"Why would they recognise me?" Alida asked in puzzlement. She was hardly a public figure, and her fame, such as it was, could only be of interest to a small section of the community.

"Stacey informs me that the girls here have a fixation about clothes. Amongst other things," Gareth replied sardonically. "From the reaction you're getting, I suspect she brought your photograph to school with her. Probably as a piece of one-upmanship."

Alida wasn't sure how to take that. "Is Stacey herself interested in fashion?" she asked warily.

"No. But I think peer-group pressure is getting to her." He heaved a rueful sigh. "That's her coming now, being clutched and whispered to."

A long-legged girl, tall for her age, and not looking at all pleased by what she was being told, Alida thought with a sinking feeling of disappointment. Stacey certainly wasn't breaking into an excited run to greet her father and his companion. If anything, her steps had slowed, and the dark frown on her face suggested that this meeting was not only unexpected, but unwelcome.

She said something with vehemence, shook off her companions and strode ahead of them, her head tilted high in haughty independence, two thick black plaits swinging their disapproval of whatever had been suggested to her. She totally ignored the huddle of girls who watched her approach with avid interest, their eyes darting from Stacey to Gareth and Alida. She skirted them and came straight towards her father, disdaining to even glance at Alida.

Any similarity to Gareth stopped at her black hair and long legs. She must take after her mother, Alida thought, noting the flashing dark eyes, the straight aristocratic little nose, the full-lipped mouth and the smooth oval chin. It was a vivid little face, and Alida felt a fierce stab of jealousy at the thought that Gareth's wife must have been a strikingly attractive woman.

She must also have been dark-haired to have left that legacy of brilliant dark eyes in her daughter. Pale skin and a high colour in her cheeks. *I'm so different in looks,* Alida thought. Was that why Gareth had chosen to use me, because I'm such a contrast to the wife he had loved? Because I couldn't remind him of her in any way whatsoever? Had that made it easier for him?

"You said you were taking *me* out," Stacey opened up in angry accusation.

"That's what I'm here for," Gareth replied curtly. "Do they teach you rudeness at this school, Stacey?"

"Then what's *she* doing here with you?" Stacey demanded, too worked up to reply to her father's reproof.

"I invited Miss Rose to meet you. I did not expect her to be greeted with such discourtesy from my daughter," he grated.

The flush on Stacey's cheeks burnt more brightly. She shot a hostile look at Alida. "I don't mind you having my father at night. But I don't get to see him very often and—"

"Stacey, get in the car!" Gareth commanded coldly. "We will not put on a show for your goggle-eyed friends."

She flounced past him and opened the front passenger door. In an instant, Gareth wheeled and had her arm in a vicelike grip, preventing her from taking the seat. "Thank you for opening the door for Miss Rose, Stacey," he said. "I'm glad to see you haven't entirely forsaken good manners. Alida..."

The girl stood there seething as Alida blindly complied with Gareth's command. He shut the door after her, then opened the back door for his daughter. Stacey got in with bad grace but no verbal protest. Alida no longer cared what the girl did or said. Her sickening words *I don't mind you having my father at night,* were eating into her heart. Gareth had discussed her with his daughter, apparently in such terms that Stacey had reason to resent Alida's sudden appearance in *her* time.

What had he said? It's nothing serious, Stacey? Just a city woman I happen to fancy? Oh, yes, very beautiful, but not the type to ever take your mother's place!

She couldn't look at Gareth as he took the driver's seat and started the engine with an angry roar. He reversed abruptly from the parking bay and accelerated out of the school grounds. The school where girls of Stacey's class were sent, the privileged, moneyed class that bought the clothes designed by Alida, but who would always consider her beneath their level of establishment society.

Only when they were on the road and into the traffic stream leading to the city centre did Gareth speak. "You will now apologise to Miss Rose, Stacey, for your incredibly rude behaviour towards her," he commanded tersely.

"You said you'd take me to the movies," came the rebellious reply. "You said—"

"I said you will damned well apologise!" he shouted over his shoulder in temper.

Mutinous silence.

"Stop the car and let me out, Gareth," Alida said quietly. It was the end. The absolute end. There was no possible hope of any future for them.

"No!" he snapped. Then he expelled a long shuddering breath and produced a calm controlled voice. "Stacey, I am not cutting you short. I do not forget my promises. I simply asked Miss Rose to join us. She wanted to meet you. I thought you might like to meet her. What, might I ask, is your problem with this arrangement?"

More mutinous silence.

"Stacey!" Impatiently.

"She doesn't fit into our lives," came the fiercely resentful reply. "Go to bed with her if you have to, but why should you want me to meet her?"

It was precisely what Alida had deduced from Stacey's behaviour towards her, yet the bald shock of the spoken words sent a wave of utter revulsion through her. Gareth was stumped for a reply. He had none, Alida's dulled brain told her. The only reason he had instituted this gambit of meeting his daughter was as a sop to her sensibilities so he could get his own way with her!

"Let me out, Gareth," she repeated more strongly. "I don't want this any more than your daughter does. She's the same as her mother!"

"*You* didn't know my mother!" Stacey sniped from the back seat. "And don't think *you* can ever take her place!"

"Stacey!" Gareth yelled, then blazed a furious look at Alida. "What the hell does that mean?"

All the pain he had given her forged her reply. Why should she spare them anything? Neither of them had given one damn about her feelings.

"Your wife didn't mind you treating me as a whore. Neither does your daughter. As long as I'm kept separated from your real lives. Which is what you want, too," Alida seethed at him. "So stop the car and let me go, Gareth! And don't ever come near me again. Because I'm through with being used as your whore!"

"Alida, no!" He shook his head. "It's not like that! I swear to you."

"Stop it! Just stop it!" she screamed. "I can't bear any more!"

He swore and thumped the driving wheel. "As soon as we're off the freeway I'll stop and we'll talk this over sensibly."

He still wasn't prepared to give up his plan. He was totally without conscience or caring where she was concerned. Only what *he* wanted mattered to him.

"What did she mean, Mummy didn't mind?" Stacey demanded.

Gareth muttered something venomous under his breath, then his mouth compressed into a hard grim line, denying any ready answer to his daughter.

"Dad?" Stacey persisted. Then with angry resentment, "You can't let her speak about Mum like that."

Alida gave a harsh bitter laugh. "But you can speak about me any way you like. As nasty and hurtful as you please."

"Alida." Gareth's eyes stabbed a plea at her but it didn't reach her heart. She had no heart left for any of the softer, kinder emotions, only a hard core that burned with a blistering demand for the unvarnished truth and a meting of some justice from the murk of how she had been treated.

"Why not answer her, Gareth?" she mocked. "Tell your daughter about your arrangement with your wife. Tell her how you used me and left me five years ago. No doubt she'll understand and approve of how you handled the situation."

"Dad?" Stacey's voice quavered uncertainly. "What's she talking about?"

"She!" Alida jeered, her mind torn by all the unanswered needs that both Gareth and Stacey had dangled in front of her. "Oh, what a good word for the other woman! Just *she!* No name! A nobody on the sidelines! Discarded after *she* has served her purpose!"

"Dad?"

"Alida! For God's sake! Stacey is only a child!" Gareth pleaded hoarsely.

It triggered another outpouring of bitterness. "Yes! A child of your wife! Your precious daughter who treats me like dirt to be swept under the mat! Just like you did."

"I had no choice then," he protested fiercely. "I promised—"

She laughed, a high, hysterical peal of derision. "Promises to your wife, promises to your daughter, but none to me. Oh, no! Don't ask for promises, Alida. Just give me what I want. After all, it's only one more hitchhiker wanting a quick ride on the fast lane. Why shouldn't I indulge you? We only live once!"

"Daddy?" Another urgent appeal from the back seat.

"Stacey, this is not how it sounds," he answered.

"Why lie to her?" Alida jeered. "You obviously have a fine understanding between you of what's important and what's not."

"I haven't lied to her," Gareth shot back furiously. "I don't know who's been filling Stacey's head with a load of rubbish, but if you'd ever had a child, you'd realise—"

The last bastion of any sensible discretion exploded, and before Alida could stop herself the most painful truth of all was spilling out. "I have a child, Gareth. The bastard son you fathered on me. But you don't know about him, do you? You didn't care enough to protect me from any consequences."

"Daddy?" It was a panicky appeal.

Alida swung around in her seat, her green eyes blazing with fathoms of uncontrollable bitterness. It was as though the madness of revealing what she should never have revealed released an even wilder madness. Words spat from her tongue in a totally destructive torrent.

"Oh, yes, Stacey! You have a brother. Or I should say half brother. And while you've enjoyed your father's devotion all the years of your life, your little half brother hasn't known a father at all. But you wouldn't care about that, either. You want your father all to yourself. Well, you keep your father all to yourself!"

"Alida!" Shock was stamped on Gareth's face, draining it of colour and drawing the flesh into stark tautness. He was suddenly breathing hard. "What the hell are you saying?"

"You have a son, Gareth!" she hurled at him. "A son you're never going to know! Because he's mine.

And just as your daughter won't let me near you, I won't let you near him!''

The blue eyes turned to her in glazed horror.

Suddenly they were all flung forward, the force of the impact coming before the sound of crunching metal. Their seat belts saved them from any serious injury but they sat dazed for several seconds before realising the Mercedes had crashed into the stationary vehicle ahead of them. A red traffic light, Alida noted belatedly. A man stepped out of the skewed and crumpled car in front of them, shaking a furious fist at Gareth.

The light turned green and other cars drove on, but they were stopped. Forcibly stopped. Alida undid her seat belt, opened the door and got out of the car.

''Alida . . .''

Gareth's voice was ragged, but she didn't look back. Her brain told her that the other driver would hold him up, demanding retribution of one kind or another. She was safe from pursuit. She felt weak and shaky from the shock of the accident and the emotional trauma of the last few minutes, but she managed to keep walking. She turned a corner and saw a taxi coming towards her. She raised her arm.

She dropped into the back seat, gave her address, then let herself go limp and closed her eyes. A phrase from the Bible slid through her mind. *Vengeance is mine, saith the Lord.* What she had done was wrong, Alida knew it was, but somehow she didn't care.

Let them suffer, she thought. Let them suffer as she and Andy had suffered, forced into a void that had no resolution. No more contempt from Gareth and his daughter. When they finished answering to each other for what they'd done, she hoped they felt as low as they had made her feel.

CHAPTER SEVEN

IT FELT LIKE a million years since she'd left Jill's office, yet Alida found it was only a little after four o'clock when she arrived home. She went mechanically about the tasks of getting ready to leave—changing into comfortable travelling clothes, packing her bag, stacking the few perishable foods into a carton, checking that all the windows and external doors were securely locked.

She notified the post office, the gardening service and the security company of her imminent departure and the expected date of her return. The post office would send her mail on. The other two services would see that her house was not burgled in her absence, that the garden and lawns were well-maintained and any junk mail was regularly removed and disposed of.

The last thing she did was make a call to Jill's apartment, perfectly aware that her friend would not be home yet. She did not want to talk to anyone. It was much easier to leave a message on Jill's answering machine. She waited for the beeps then spoke quickly.

"It's Alida. I'm going home, Jill. If anything vitally important crops up, let me know. Otherwise I won't be back for two months. All the best with everything. Bye for now.''

Satisfied that she had taken care of everything, Alida locked the door leading from the house to the garage behind her and climbed into a big four-wheel drive Range Rover.

For where she was going, it was the ideal vehicle. High enough off the ground to avoid the crown of sand that built up between wheel tracks, and built to withstand the punishment of corrugated roads and rough treatment, which could result in broken springs and mechanical failures in less durable vehicles, the Range Rover would go where no other vehicle could go.

Alida had been planning this trip for a while. Now that the fashion awards were over, there was nothing to stop her from leaving. She had meant to go this weekend, or next weekend, anyway. Only Gareth could have kept her here. This afternoon's events had demonstrated how futile that would have been.

Over the past week Alida had checked through all the equipment necessary for the long trip ahead of her. She was well-prepared for all types of breakdowns and emergencies. Such precautions were second nature to her. The Outback was an unforgiving terrain to the careless and inexperienced traveller. A garage mechanic and auto electrician had given everything a thorough inspection, and when Alida switched on the motor, the steady thrum was like music to her ears. It was the sound of freedom from all city cares.

The garage door was operated by a remote control device. Alida felt a grim satisfaction as it lowered and locked after she had driven out. If Gareth Morgan did try coming to talk *sensibly* to her, he would be waiting a long time for any sign of life from this house. She hoped he burned with frustration. Which wasn't nice of her, but he and his daughter had soured all her niceness.

It was a relief when she finally left the city and all its traffic behind her. The Great Northern Highway stretched ahead of her, eight hundred kilometres of bitumen road to Meekatharra before she turned inland towards the infamous Gunbarrel Highway that ran as straight as a die through the heart of the Great Sandy Desert.

For quick visits to her home, Alida flew the distance. For her twice-yearly retreats she took the Range Rover all the way. Then she needed the mobility the vehicle gave her so that she could immerse herself in the life and landscape that had always been her inspiration. Both were unique and primitive. By the time she returned to Perth she would have all the ideas she needed for her winter or summer collection, whichever she was working on.

As she drove farther and farther north, Alida felt she was shrugging off sophisticated civilisation. Western Australian was like that, she reflected. Despite its immense area, covering more than two and a half million square kilometres, three quarters of its small population lived in or near its capital city. It was still the Frontier State, with its scattered homesteads, vast distances and rich mineral deposits. It was mainly the gold rushes of the old days that had brought progress in Western Australia, but it was the land—always the land—that dominated it.

The sheep and cattle station that Alida's family owned was nowhere near as big as Gareth Morgan's Riordan River Station. Nor as prosperous. But they made a reasonable living out of it in the good years. Drought, of course, was always the enemy. The soil was not bad. It simply lacked water. Feed was sparse in the dry years when only the underground bores kept them going. Yet it was the kind of life that seeped into a person's soul and held them captive. Alida knew her parents would never give it up. Neither would her two younger brothers.

If she hadn't been a girl, if her mother hadn't been so committed to giving her every opportunity to develop her artistic talents, if so many sacrifices hadn't been made on her behalf, sacrifices Alida felt constrained to repay by striving for success, then she would never have made her life in the city.

Her parents were proud of all she'd done and achieved. How could she deny them that pleasure? She kept a foot in their world even if she couldn't share it completely. It was probably better this way, Alida thought despondently.

Her brothers wouldn't have liked her bossing them around. That had been all right when they were kids, but they were grown up now with tough individual attitudes of their own. By the time she had finished school, their positions in the family had been reversed, with the boys being given the more important responsibilities. Gone were the days when her parents had said, "Alida can do it." Or "You boys do what Alida tells you."

Apart from that, she did enjoy designing, and it meant that her brothers would inherit the station. Where there were men to carry on, that was the natural order of things. Of course, she would always have a home there. She could stay as long as she liked, and whenever she wanted to. But the expectation had been that she would get married one day and go wherever her husband took her. Life ran along very simple lines in Outback country.

One very simple rule was: do what has to be done. Gareth had said that this afternoon, except he had assumed he could depend on his daughter to follow his lead. That had backfired on him. His daughter didn't want Alida taking her mother's place. Well, that was fine, Alida thought bitterly, because Gareth didn't want her taking Kate's place, either. An affair on the side was all he wanted her for.

Tears blurred her eyes. She hastily wiped them away. She would not cry over Gareth Morgan. Never again. She and Andy were better off without him. And his brat of a daughter!

Alida drove until her eyes were smarting with fatigue. She stopped at a roadside diner obviously popular with the truck drivers, since several big rigs were

pulled up outside. She ordered a hamburger and
French fries, knowing she needed the sustenance to
keep going. The waitress was cheerful and talkative
and the serving was more than generous. The plate
overflowed with French fries and Alida could hardly
get her mouth around the hamburger, which was piled
high with fried onions and bacon as well as the usual
salad accompaniments.

Surprisingly it aroused her appetite, and Alida
thoroughly enjoyed her meal. She eavesdropped on
the truckies' rather loud conversation, smiled at their
ribald jokes and good-humoured patter with the
waitress. Somehow it eased her inner misery, bringing
things back to normal.

Long ago, when she was a child, the Aborigines had
taught her that you either laughed at life and learned
to flow with it, or you fought it and went mad. Of
course, they had been talking about accepting and
empathising with their life and land. The city didn't
breed that sense of togetherness with the environ-
ment. But already the city was a long way behind her.

She drank two cups of coffee, then feeling much
more relaxed and refreshed, she set off again, hoping
to do a few more hours' driving before she had to stop
and sleep.

Whether the meal had relaxed her too much, or the
lack of restful sleep last night was catching up with
her, Alida didn't know, but she found her eyes glaz-
ing again all too soon. Knowing it was stupid to fight
it, she pulled into the next lay-by along the highway.

The air mattress and blankets were all ready for her in the back of the Range Rover, and Alida was asleep within seconds of settling herself.

The morning light woke her. She drove on to the next fuel stop, filled up her petrol tank, used the rest room for a wash and tidy up, grabbed a cup of coffee and was back on the highway within half an hour. The last stretch to Meekatharra was no hardship to Alida. The thought of getting closer and closer to home was heart-lifting.

There had been some early spring rains, and on either side of the road, countless millions of pink and white everlasting daisies stretched as far as the eye could see. This was wild flower country, and Alida knew there were over four thousand plant species in this arid wonderland, but they needed rain to make them bloom. It had been a good year, one of the best ever, and the flowers reflected the ideal conditions.

She stopped in Meekatharra for breakfast and to refuel for the last leg of the journey.

Meekatharra was a small quiet town, yet it was an important centre of supplies and services for the inland. It was one of the bases for the Royal Flying Doctor Service in Western Australia, as well as the School of the Air, which had directed all Alida's correspondence lessons before she was sent away to boarding school in Perth.

Being at Meekatharra always brought back fond memories of the camp schools she had attended, when all the children from the stations in the areas were billoted in town for two weeks a year. This was to give them a taste of real classroom lessons, as well as the opportunity to mix and play with each other. They had been good times—the highlight of the year in some ways—yet Alida was always glad to get home. A town was interesting to visit, but she never envied the town children their life.

There were two hundred kilometres left to travel, most of it towards Wiluna before turning off on the station track to the homestead. This was all dirt road, which meant driving at a much lower speed, but Alida didn't mind. The closer she got to home, the more content she felt.

The rich red earth, the mulga trees, the stunted desert acacia, the yellow daisies and purple pigface splashing colour over the rolling plains, the occasional clumps of ghost gums marking waterholes and the rocky outcrops of sandstone, striated and shimmering with desert colours in the white-hot sunshine, a herd of wild camels in the distance, idly grazing on edible trees and shrubs—all of it was part of the magic for Alida.

I can forget Gareth here, she thought. *He and his daughter will fade into inconsequential pieces of the past that won't matter any more. Andy and I will share our life. I don't need any part of them.*

The thought of her son brought a smile of happy anticipation. Two weeks ago she had flown him up to Meekatharra, and her parents had met them there and taken him home with them, only too happy to mind him for her during the busy time leading up to the awards presentation. It would be so good to hug Andy in her arms again and listen to his little-boy chatter as he told her all that had happened to him during his adventures with Grandpa and Grandma.

It was a joy to finally reach the turn-off to Rose Station. There was no sign, no gate, no fence, only a track leading off into the wilderness, yet to Alida it was as familiar as the back of her hand. Eventually she came to gates and fences but they were few and far between. In good country, twenty thousand acres would carry twenty thousand sheep or more. Here in the Outback, the same number of sheep needed seven hundred and fifty thousand acres, and the station owner only saw his full stock twice a year at muster.

Then at last the homestead with all its outbuildings came into view, and Alida recklessly accelerated, uncaring of the bumps and potholes. She might not have noticed the plane sitting on the rough homestead airstrip except for its whiteness glinting in the sun. It looked like a new plane and an expensive one. A six-seater Cessna if she was not mistaken. Which meant visitors.

She wondered who of her parents' or brothers' friends could afford such a sleek machine, then shrugged away the speculation. It could be someone who was lost. Navigation was tricky when the land looked the same for hundreds and hundreds of kilometres. In any event, as far as Alida was concerned, it didn't matter who it was. She was home, back where she belonged, once more safe in the heart of her family who loved her.

Her mother was on the veranda, waving to her as Alida drove up to the house, a cloud of red dust churned up behind her. Her mother—still tall and straight and indomitable. The house—hardly an elegant structure, rather ramshackle with the additions made over the years, but solid and spacious and practical for the hot dry climate that prevailed most of the year.

Alida brought the Range Rover to a halt at the front steps, leapt out of the high cabin and bounced around the vehicle in sheer exuberance. She did not notice that the smile of welcome on Mary Rose's face was somewhat strained. She looked for Andy to be on the veranda with his grandmother but her quick scan was stopped dead by the two people who had no right to be there!

Her feet faltered in midstep. Alida could feel her heart catapulting around her chest as Gareth Morgan rose from the cane armchair in which he had been sitting, determined purpose stamped on his face. Stacey Morgan hastily stood and pressed herself to her father's side, looking anxiously at both him and Alida.

The plane. Alida's stunned mind slowly made the connection. Somehow Gareth had found out where she was headed and had flown here ahead of her. The shock of seeing him suddenly gave way to sickening panic. Her eyes flew to her mother's.

"Where's Andy?"

"Not here, Alida," she answered quietly, her lined and weathered face creased in concern. "He went out with your father and brothers early this morning. They're fixing the fence on the eastern run."

Alida almost sagged with relief. Gareth hadn't met Andy yet. Nothing irreparable had been said or done. Except her mother now knew who was Andy's father. The knowledge was written in the strained look in her eyes.

Gareth had obviously not minced his words in announcing exactly who he was and why he was here. Gareth Morgan did what had to be done. Alida silently cursed herself for not realising he would leave no stone unturned to find *his* son. She should never have told him. It had been a crazy thing to do. Her mind frantically sought escape routes from the consequences of her reckless revelation.

Could she lie? Could she say she had flung her child in his face to hurt him as he had hurt her? Could she say Andy wasn't his at all? Would Gareth accept that and go away before Andy returned home?

Not Gareth Morgan, she decided. He had flown all the way up here to see the child. He would want to see. He would check dates. He would arrive at certain conclusions, then he would stake his claim.

Alida heaved a defeated sigh and forced her feet forward and up the steps to the veranda. "I'm sorry, Mum," she murmured as she kissed her cheek. Then she managed an apologetic smile. "I didn't mean to bring this trouble on you."

"What's done is done, Alida," Mary Rose replied, her eyes soft with understanding. It was another simple rule. Accept what cannot be changed. Do the best you can from here.

She patted Alida's cheek in a comforting gesture. "I'll make you a cup of tea while you talk to your visitors."

Which left Alida facing Gareth and his daughter. Stacey, in T-shirt and jeans, looked younger and more vulnerable than she had in her tailored school uniform. Gareth looked more formidable than ever. He had discarded the leather jacket he had worn yesterday, and his strong physique was all the more evident with only a fine white shirt and the fawn moleskins covering him. Despite everything that had happened, Alida still could not deny the force of his attraction. It was wrong, all wrong, she thought, but an ache started in her stomach and spread to her limbs.

Andy's father...

Stacey's father first and foremost, she reminded herself savagely.

She eyed both father and daughter with bitter mockery. "Who told you I was coming here? I can't believe you found your way by instinct."

"I persuaded Jill Masters to reveal your whereabouts," Gareth replied matter-of-factly. "Since she would only tell me that your family lived on a station somewhere beyond Meekatharra, I flew to the airport there and made some inquiries at the Flying Doctor base. One of their pilots located the homestead on a map for me."

"Elementary," Alida conceded dryly. For someone like him. "I'm amazed that your daughter is with you. Hasn't she already witnessed enough, Gareth?"

"Miss Rose." Stacey answered for herself, her vivid face flushed with what looked like agonised self-consciousness. "I wanted to…to apologise for the way I behaved yesterday. It was very mean."

"Yes, it was mean, Stacey."

"I'm sorry. Truly, desperately sorry."

Alida silently but sceptically challenged the apology. The girl held her gaze unflinchingly, the dark eyes pleading forgiveness. It was Alida who looked away, her emotions beginning to churn in turmoil again. Her eyes sought familiar landmarks around the homestead, instinctively wanting to find the sense of peace and harmony this place had always instilled in her. But there was no peace with Gareth and his daughter here.

"Alida, you knew I had to come," Gareth said softly.

"Yes. I suppose I knew that," she murmured. But not here. Not so soon. She wasn't ready to deal with the consequences of yesterday's raw disclosure. She had locked it out of her mind, wanting, needing to believe it didn't change anything.

She watched two pink-breasted galahs swoop down to the water trough next to the well that serviced the house. The birds led a simple life, following a natural cycle, she thought. Water, food, nesting, mating. Why couldn't her life be that simple?

But she herself had made his mess, and there was no escaping from it. Such a destructive loss of control, leaving Andy open to the same kind of hurt she had suffered at the Morgans' hands! How best to protect him from it? That was the question now. It was paramount that she stay calm, not lose her head again, not let *them* get under her skin. She had to keep control of this encounter.

She turned to Gareth, an ironic little smile curling her lips. ''Just as I know you haven't come to see me. Either of you.'' She gestured towards the chairs. ''But please sit down. The Rose family prides itself on generous hospitality. We won't treat you any differently.''

''Will you sit with us?'' Gareth asked, his blue eyes trying to probe the depth of her hostility towards them.

''Of course. We don't turn anyone away here. Not even the scoundrels,'' Alida answered, her eyes mocking his concern.

They both waited until she had seated herself. The cane furniture was old and squeaky. Alida remembered her father buying it for her mother the Christmas she was ten years old. The wide veranda was a favourite place to sit and watch the sunset when the day's work was done. It had been a good year, the year she was ten.

''When did you arrive?'' she asked.

"A couple of hours ago," Gareth answered.

"I expect you'll be staying the night then."

"Your mother kindly offered us rooms." He paused, then slowly added, "She's been telling us about your life here, Alida."

"If you'd looked at what I create, my life here is woven into every design," Alida said, not letting him see her bitter resentment at his lack of interest and his lack of perception in branding her a loose-living city woman. "The geometrical pattern on the culotte I'm wearing is derived from Aboriginal drawings in one of the caves on this station. The grey-green of my pullover is the colour of the spinifex that is the main vegetation of the inland."

"I'm sorry. I hadn't noticed that kind of detail," he said quietly.

Alida dismissed his answer with a shrug. "Most men don't."

"It's . . . it's very clever," Stacey offered nervously.

Alida found it difficult to look at Gareth's daughter with any semblance of equanimity, but she forced herself to acknowledge the comment. "There are obviously some people who think so."

The words came out so coldly that the girl shrank back into her chair and bit her lips. Her eyes darted to her father, imploring his guidance. He had undoubtedly coached her for *this* meeting, Alida cynically decided. Stacey was obviously frightened of putting any foot wrong today.

Gareth, however, wasn't watching his daughter. His gaze was fastened on Alida, seeing the hard pride on her smooth beautiful face, the flat rejection in her green eyes, the wall she was putting between them.

"How far is it to the eastern run?" he asked.

Alida regarded him balefully. "Thinking of walking, Gareth?"

"No. I was thinking of driving. The vehicle you came in should take us wherever we have to go. The sooner we get this situation sorted out, the better." He stood up. "I suggest you come with me so that we can discuss what's best to be done before you introduce me to *our* son."

Alida came out of her chair, fighting mad at his arrogant assumption of authority. "You think you can commandeer my Range Rover? Just like that? Order me around as though you're in charge of everything? Well, let me tell you, Gareth Morgan, you're going to have very little say in *my* son's life!"

The determination carved on his face remained rocklike. There was not one flicker of uncertainty in the blazing blue eyes. "You prefer to sit around all afternoon, Alida?" he challenged. "What good purpose will that serve? Do you want *our* son to walk into the kind of hostile atmosphere you're creating here?"

"*I'm* not creating it," she denied hotly, but he had a point, Alida privately conceded. She was still off-balance at being confronted by Gareth and his daughter in her own home. She hadn't even begun to think ahead to their meeting with Andy.

"I realise you must be tired of driving," Gareth pressed on. "It will be easier on you if you sit in the passenger seat and direct me."

"Fine! I have quite a lot of direction to give you, Gareth," Alida bit out, determined to regain the initiative.

He turned to his daughter. "Stacey, stay here. I wish to get things settled with Alida."

"Yes, Dad," she muttered in a tone of flat resignation.

No joy there, Alida thought. No joy anywhere. "If you'll excuse me for a few moments," she said coldly. "I'll let my mother know what we're doing."

She turned her back on both of them and strode inside the house. As well as informing her mother, she needed to go to the bathroom before setting out on another rough trip. A splash of cold water might also help to bring her to her senses.

Her pulse was thrumming in her temples. Her stomach was fluttering with nerves. All at the thought of being alone with Gareth Morgan! It was crazy to feel this way about him. Crazy to let him get to her on any level whatsoever. She had to stop it somehow, or the future was going to consist of a long line of bitter miseries.

CHAPTER EIGHT

ALIDA GRUDGINGLY CONCEDED that Gareth drove with instinctive competence over the treacherous terrain that took them to the eastern run. He automatically avoided the red sand dunes where they might have bogged. He skirted potholes and rocks without abusing the steerage or the brakes, and managed to keep a steady pace overall. With his experience of the Outback, it was only to be expected, but Alida was still niggled that he handled the vehicle as well, if not better, than she did.

"You said you wanted to talk to me," she reminded him after they had travelled for twenty minutes with nothing forthcoming from him and only terse navigational instructions from her.

"I'm thinking about it," he replied. Which did nothing to ease the thick tension in the cabin.

"It doesn't seem to be very productive," Alida sniped, impatient and frustrated with his prolonged silence.

"It's about time to take a little detour," he said enigmatically but decisively.

Alida threw him a vexed look, but his eyes were concentrated on picking the best route ahead. Then, contrary to her directions, he swung the Range Rover towards the creek bed to the north of them.

"You're off track," she snapped.

"It's always rather peaceful, looking at water," he replied in a maddeningly calm voice.

Alida opened her mouth to tell him that this creek bed was a dry one, except when it rained. She promptly shut her mouth again when she realised precisely where he was heading. With unerring judgment Gareth had picked out the one permanent waterhole.

It was where the ghost gums grew the tallest, where there was a profusion of tea-trees, where the deep green vegetation was backed by a freakish rock strata, which ran in great buttresses and giant steps. It was, coincidentally, one of her favourite places on the station.

Gareth brought the Range Rover to a halt well short of the sandy creek bank. He grabbed one of her blankets from the back of the vehicle before coming around to open Alida's door. She eyed the blanket with heart-pumping suspicion. Did Gareth have more in mind than talking?

"This might take some time," he said dryly. "We can sit in the shade by the water."

"There are rocks we can sit on," she informed him just as dryly.

A taunting amusement glittered in his eyes. "Not for me, thank you, Alida. But you make your own choice."

"I intend to," she warned him.

She consciously kept a comfortable distance between herself and Gareth as they walked to the waterhole. All her instincts were shrieking that this was a dangerous situation and she had to keep her head. When Gareth spread out the blanket she moved aside, leaning her back against the trunk of the largest tree, watching him from under her lashes.

He was not as relaxed as he looked, she decided, despite the graceful economy of his every movement. He had rolled up his shirt sleeves, and the muscles in his forearms were taut as he straightened the blanket. His powerful thighs strained against the cloth of his trousers. She looked away, remembering all too well the feel of those thighs against her own.

The waterhole was about fifteen metres long and seven metres wide. She and her brothers had often swum and played here in the heat of the day, but this was no time for playing. What was about to transpire between Gareth and herself was deadly serious. Alida had to protect her rights as Andy's mother and the only parent her son had known up until now.

"What's Andy like, Alida?" Gareth asked quietly.

She flicked a glance at him. He had not sat down. Nor had he stepped towards her. He stood with his legs apart, his hands resting loosely on his hips. There was an animal quality of stillness about him, his whole being concentrated on watching every minute response from her. Watching and waiting for his moment to move in on her, Alida thought wildly.

She looked at the rocks on the other side of the waterhole, as old as time and just as unfeeling, sentinels to the futility of fighting what cannot be changed. Accept it, Alida, she told herself. Gareth was not going to go away. Ever. Not for her, nor for all the restless yearnings he evoked in her, and not for Andy, who should be allowed to love his father.

"A normal four-year-old," she said shortly.

He looked at her patiently, waiting for more.

"He's beautiful," she said at last, truthfully. A smile teased at her lips as she thought of her son. "Endlessly inquisitive, too adventurous for his own good, noisy, full of the excitement of life."

"Has he asked about me?"

Alida grimaced. "He asked why he doesn't have a father."

"What did you reply?"

She shot Gareth a defensive look but found no aggressive resentment in his eyes, only a patient watchfulness. "I pointed out that he had a grandfather and two uncles and not everyone can have a father, as well. He seemed content with that answer. He spends a lot of time up here so it's not as if he hasn't had any male companionship and caring."

She hoped Gareth got the message that Andy wasn't in *need* of him. He was perfectly happy with the family he had.

"Jill Masters said that you retreat here for four months of the year."

"At a minimum. More than that usually. Andy loves the life on the station," Alida added with a touch of defiance. Gareth couldn't offer her son anything that she didn't already give him. Andy was certainly not a deprived child in any sense whatsoever.

"Wouldn't Riordan River serve just as well, Alida?"

Shock rippled through her. She searched his eyes in alarm. Intense and unwavering purpose stared back at her. "You can't mean you want Andy with you all the time," she cried in vehement protest. "You can't expect so much. It's not fair!"

"Alida..." He winced, took a deep breath, and the blue eyes bored into hers. "I meant for you to be with him, as well."

"Oh, that would be really good!" she replied sarcastically. "Just like old times!"

He winced again. "I'm asking you to marry me."

It was like a punch to the heart. The pain of such cynical calculation was agonising. Her stomach contracted. She felt herself begin to shake. There was a buzzing in her ears. Somehow she found the strength to push away from the tree, to walk away from him, away from the proposal that would have made her the happiest woman in the world. If it had been offered with love.

Alida's feet seemed totally disassociated from the rest of her body. They were directed by a terrible shrieking in her mind. Even when they staggered in the soft sand, they were still driven on, impelled by her need for solitude, the need for time to lick her emotional wounds, to gather her pride and stiffen her backbone.

"Alida..."

A harsh urgent cry, echoing in her head, like the echoes of dreams that had never been fulfilled, never would be fulfilled. Birds flew away at the strident sound, all the birds with their simple lives. It was right for them to fly away, to leave behind the ugly mess of human emotions. What carefree creature would want to witness that?

Hands gripped her upper arms, held her steady.

"Let go of me, Gareth!" Was that raw sound her voice?

She felt the heat emanating from his body, the tensile strength of his hands, his reluctance to release her.

"Then don't turn your back on me, Alida," he rasped.

"Why not? You think that option is exclusively yours, Gareth?"

The heave of his breath fanned her ear. Alida felt a deep primitive satisfaction at having delivered that counterpunch. She savoured the passion of hatred with a feverish exultation. It flourished in the barren ground that had been her love for him.

"Get this straight, Alida!" His voice was low and grim, and throbbing with passion. "I'm through with feeling guilty about you. It's the future we have to look at, not the past. And I am not going to carry around a load of guilt for the rest of my life! When all's said and done, I didn't do a damned thing you didn't want me to do!''

He dropped his grip on her arms. "So what do you want now, Alida?" he taunted. "If it's a fight, I'll give you one. Because I'm not walking away this time. And you can't, either.''

Adrenalin shot violent energy through her body. She spun around and faced him, her chin tilted at a rebellious angle, her green eyes glittering with fierce pride. "Well, you can forget marriage for a start, Gareth," she flung at him.

"It's the best solution," he argued.

"For you it is. You think I can't see the future you've got mapped out in your calculating mind? Marriage, divorce, with the subsequent legal claim on my son?''

"*Your* son. And divorce does not figure in my mind, Alida.''

She laughed at him. "How do you expect us to become one big happy family, Gareth?''

"We work at it," he said grimly.

"Well, try working at it before you propose marriage to me," she taunted. "I don't want to be stepmother to a girl who hates the thought of me taking her mother's place. Nor do I want a husband who sees me only as a sexual convenience. Why on earth should I put myself in such a position, when by staying free of you I hold the upper hand where Andy is concerned?''

"You're not free of me, Alida." The blue eyes glittered into hers with arrogant certainty. "Any more than I'm free of you."

He didn't mean the tie of having a child between them. He stood there, insultingly confident in his sexuality, which played havoc with all her senses, deliberately challenging her with the deeply primitive desire not even hatred could quench.

"I'll listen to reasonable terms," she snapped, her nerves wire tight under the derisive simmer in his eyes.

"This isn't a reasonable situation. You know it. I know it," he softly jeered. "You came with me to meet Stacey yesterday because you wanted marriage, Alida. So now we set about making it feasible."

"No!"

"Yes!"

Alida's heart gave a violent leap as she saw Gareth's control disintegrate. There was no time to evade him. He reached for her, scooped her hard against the heated desire of his powerful body. Raw naked want blazed from his eyes.

"You want me as much as I want you," he grated, his face working with intense emotion. One hand held her with rocklike steadiness. The other wove through her hair, controlling the tilt of her head.

"No, I don't," she defied him.

"Then walk away from me. For good. And then we'll fight our fight for the rest of our lives."

That sobered Alida's bitter rebellion. Gareth would fight her, and fight her over Andy, for the rest of her life. Whether she liked it or not, their lives were now intertwined.

"I don't totally detest having you holding me," she conceded.

"That's what I thought," he said grimly, his head bending towards hers.

"But this is not the time or the place," she argued wildly.

"Yes it is," he disagreed.

His mouth took hers with passion, an invasion so fast and ravaging in its need to take and possess that Alida was lost without another blow being struck in defence. Her stunned surrender to his desperate need for her lasted only seconds. Then it was as though all the emotional inhibitions that had festered in her mind over the last few days were torn apart by a rampaging need to take what she could of him. There was no rational thought involved. It was a madness that knew only a craving that had to be answered.

Her arms coiled over his tautly muscled shoulders. Her hands clutched his head, her fingers revelling in the thick silky texture of his hair. She kissed him with the same urgent devouring hunger that had ravished her mouth.

There was no seductive finesse in what followed, no sophisticated lead-in to lovemaking, nothing at all civilised in the clawing off of clothes that were an intolerable barrier to the call of the wild that coursed through their veins. Soft flesh yielded to hard, each body demanding satisfaction from the other, touch, feel, wanting, wanting, wanting. Eyes glazed with the greed of rediscovery, the sheer barbaric majesty of naked man, the softly fashioned curves of enticing womanhood.

A deep animal growl issued from Gareth's throat as he swung Alida off her feet and carried her to the blanket. Her breasts rubbed against the heaving wall of his chest. She could feel the ripple of his stomach muscles as his powerful legs strode the short distance. Her excitement was so intense she took temporary satisfaction in kissing the line of his clenched jaw, teasing at the control that had commanded a more habitable mating place than rocks and sand.

He knelt over her as he laid her down, and Alida felt a savage thrill at the desire-driven tension etched on his face and body. She parted her lips invitingly and his mouth crashed down on hers, drinking in all she would give him as though he was dying for it.

His eyes glittered at her as his hands stroked down her throat, master of the life force that beat there. They circled her breasts, lifting them, savouring their soft fullness, shaping them to his will, exulting in the thrusting peaks that quivered for his touch. He bent and drew on each of them with his mouth, a possessive sucking that shot such strong arrows of sensation through Alida that her body arched upwards and she cried out in mindless yearning. He displayed no inclination to assuage her need, nor any control—or knew none.

He fed on her breasts with ravaging passion, with the same intense wanting with which he had fed on her mouth, igniting a fierce pleasure-pain that was so exquisite and excruciating Alida felt he was consuming the inner essence of her, dragging it into his mouth, tasting it, savouring it, swallowing it. She wanted it to go on. She wanted it to stop. Her hands plucked at his head and clutched it in convulsive movements that knew no resolution. Her body writhed in a storm of sweet aching sensation.

He left her breasts throbbing with need. She opened her eyes. There was a look of intense satisfaction on his face, a wild pagan gloating in his eyes, a savage elation in his power over her. Alida reached out and trailed her fingernails down his chest. Blue fire leapt out at her. His whole body shuddered. She laughed with mad exultation, but the laughter choked in her throat as he lowered his body over hers in total domination, taking her hands in his, threading his fingers through hers, holding her arms out on either side of her.

Then his eyes closed. He rested his forehead on hers, and for several pulsating seconds their minds beat to the tunes of their bodies as they imprinted their man-woman messages on each other, the accelerated rhythm of their breathing, hearts pounding in anticipation, skin pressed to skin, vibrant with electric sensitivity, muscle contracting against muscle, a crescendo of need building to shrieking point.

Instinctively they moved in unison, driven by a blind mutual urgency that knew nothing else but the inner world that held them both in thrall, the burning core of yearning that had to be reached and soothed.

Alida wound her legs around Gareth's hips as he reared back to take the final plunge. She opened dark swimming eyes, wanting to see what he felt as he drove himself deep inside her. Yet she didn't see. All her senses were blurred by the flood of feeling that surged through her as he filled the dark loneliness of her life with the vibrant throb of his.

She moved to the beat of his need, floating beyond self, beyond time and place and circumstances, flowing with his rhythm, her entire being focused on the drumming pleasure of possession that said she belonged to him, had to belong to him, did belong to him, would always belong to him, indivisible forever and ever because that was the only way it could be.

She unwound her legs from him and placed her feet on the ground beside Gareth's knees so she could lever her hips upwards, make her own rhythm against his stroking. It filled some need. *This is so wanton,* she thought, and I'm totally decadent, but I don't care. I'm doing what I want to do because I'm me, and only he has ever made me feel like this.

The voluptuous roll of her hips excited him into a faster, wilder stroking. Low moaning noises came from his throat. I'll make him mine, mine forever, Alida promised herself, and felt her body suffuse with sweet contentment, again and again as Gareth plunged towards his ultimate climax. She felt the surge of his body, the wild rough gasping of his breath as he lowered himself to fully cover her. Then his arms wound around her and he rolled onto his side, pulling Alida with him so that they lay entwined in close intimacy.

For Alida it was sweet heaven, lying with Gareth like this. She hadn't meant to let him take her but she had, and she didn't regret it. Could this overwhelming desire sustain a marriage? Would Gareth always want her? Or was it the five years of celibacy that made his desire for her so acute?

Her mind whirled with uncertainties. But lining up strongly against the doubts was one pulsing certainty. *I don't want to be alone again. I want him with me. I want all I can have of him.*

But that was entirely selfish, Alida chided herself, even as the need and want throbbed through her whole being. The situation wasn't that simple. Whatever she did with Gareth affected other lives besides her own. She could not ignore realities that made a happy life with Gareth Morgan utterly impossible. She was not that much of a fool.

He wasn't hers. He never had been. Except perhaps in the heat of passion, when driving need obliterated every other consideration. Yet Alida could not bring herself to break the sense of togetherness she felt with him, however false and fleeting it was. All those harsh realities could wait, she argued to herself. If nothing else, she would have *now* with him, however stupid and selfish and wanton that might be. Now might be all she would ever have.

CHAPTER NINE

THE BIRDS CAME BACK, twittering onto the branches of the trees. They understood mating and nesting, Alida thought.

She placed the palm of her hand against Gareth's heart, wishing she knew what he was thinking, yet loath to break the silence between them. Her mind kept shying away from admitting anything except the reality of being together like this.

His heartbeat was slowly steadying to a normal pace. Her slight movement seemed to stir him. His hand trailed down the curve of her back, a sensual fingertip caress that made her shiver with pleasure. He softly stroked her skin, savouring its texture and the womanly shape of her body.

Very gently he lowered her onto the blanket and raised himself on one elbow, looking down at her, his face relaxed, his eyes shimmering with languorous satisfaction. He bent his head and sipped at her lips, teasing little tastes that prolonged the lingering aftermath of delicious sensitivity. His hand grazed over her stomach, her thighs, working slowly inwards to take a tender possession of her womanhood.

She looked into his eyes, saw that he wanted her again, and surrendered to his desire. Less urgently this time, more languorous, intensely sensual, perhaps even sweeter than before because they watched each other, and the pleasure of seeing each other's pleasure gave a satisfaction that heightened all their senses.

"Tell me..." Gareth's voice was furred with all he was feeling. "The man you wanted to marry...was it like this with him, Alida?"

"It's only ever been like this with you, Gareth," she answered without hesitation.

Whether it had been ego or curiosity that had prompted his question, Alida didn't know or care. She didn't have to be told that what they were so intimately sharing was special to him. The wonder of it was in his eyes, and Alida felt a deep thrill of satisfaction that Kate had not given him what she could. Not, at least, in a sexual sense. He wouldn't look like this, want like this, if it was like anything else he had ever known.

Her reply gave him satisfaction, too. His mouth slowly curved into a teasing smile, which revelled in the power he had to please her. "Can you say you've had enough of it, Alida?"

"No," she admitted. Right at this moment, she didn't care if it was shameless. Apart from which, there was one part of her mind—or heart—that wanted to know the extent of her power over him. "How often is enough for you?"

A glint of ruthless purpose came into his eyes. "I'll tell you when we're married."

There were no more words as he swiftly took her with him on a rollercoaster of overwhelming sensation. It was only when they were relaxing afterwards that Alida's mind gradually started groping around the possibility of a marriage with Gareth, wanting to believe it could work somehow.

"You really are serious about marrying me?" she asked.

"Yes." Firm and unequivocal. Apparently there were no doubts in his mind about the course of action he had set himself.

"There are a few problems," Alida reminded him.

"Such as?"

She hesitated, frowning at his careless dismissal of every other consideration. She levered herself up to look at his face. "Stacey," she said, watching for some sign of concern.

The arrogant confidence in his blue eyes did not waver in the slightest. "Basically she's a good kid."

Her lips curled in soft irony. "Even good kids can be disturbed by changes. Do you honestly expect her to accept me because of Andy?"

"I've explained the situation to her." He paused, then added, "I told her that I intend to marry you. She agrees that I should."

"What she agrees to in her mind is not necessarily what she agrees to in her heart," Alida pointed out.

The blue eyes flashed with immutable purpose. "Stacey will have to learn to live with it, and she will, Alida. I know my daughter. Yesterday she had been upset by stupid girls teasing her. I told you she was still unsettled by being away from home. And by missing her mother. The way she acted wasn't like her at all. As I said, she's basically a good kid. Apart from which, I don't intend to allow anything to stand in the way of our getting married."

"And when did you decide that, Gareth?" she asked with some asperity.

His mouth twitched in an amused smile. "About the time I asked you to dance with me at the designer awards presentation."

She stared at him, her thoughts splintering into chaos. He couldn't have had his mind made up then. She remembered his telling her he didn't know where it would lead. Unless... Could he have meant he didn't know if she would accept marriage with him?

"You didn't know about Andy then," she said, wanting to know more.

"No."

"Does that make a difference?"

"It made me more determined."

It also gave him more leverage to get her to marry him, Alida realised. "And you see no difficulties?" she queried.

"A lot."

But he didn't care, Alida thought. The words she had hurled at him yesterday suddenly took on a different meaning. *You only live once.* He had obviously decided that he was not going to die without knowing her as much as he wanted to know her. It was also clear, from what had transpired this afternoon, he felt completely satisfied with that decision.

"Do I simply come with the child?" she inquired.

He gave a mocking little laugh. "There is nothing simple about any of it, Alida. This is hardly the ideal marriage situation with us living apart half the time. But maybe we can improve on that as time goes on. At least we have more in common than I thought we had, and that's all to the good."

"You mean I know about life in the slow lane," she said dryly. There was nothing slower than the pace of life on an Outback station. Time was almost meaningless, and patience an art form.

Gareth's eyes probed hers with sharp intensity. "There never was a fast lane for you, was there, Alida?"

"No. Except in so far as I applied myself to the necessary pace of my business."

"What we had five years ago was out of the ordinary for you," he stated more than asked.

"Very much out of the ordinary."

"It didn't occur to me to ask about precautions. I am sorry about that, Alida," he said quietly.

"You didn't ask today, either."

A twinkle enlivened the blue of his eyes. "You have this effect on me. Besides, since we're getting married, I don't mind if we have another child."

Alida had the sudden and forceful impression that Gareth would have tried anything and everything to get his way with her, including making her pregnant. "What if I mind?" she asked.

He cocked a quizzical eyebrow at her. "Is it a problem?"

"No. Not this time. And I haven't said I'll marry you."

"But you're going to," he insisted.

Alida took a deep breath. Her thoughts were running wild. Perhaps Gareth felt more for her than she had ever given him credit for. After all, she had been the only woman who had overridden the strong loyalty he felt to his wife. She tried to control the fluttering hope in her heart as she asked the question that begged to be asked.

"Do you love me, Gareth?"

"Does it matter?"

"I'd like to know."

He hesitated fractionally, shrugged his shoulders. "I don't really know what I feel," he said, dismissing the subject.

"Why not?" she persisted.

He looked her directly in the eyes. "You confuse me. Always have. You're different. Nothing like I'd ever thought or expected. But I have only to look at you to feel intensely alive, Alida. And having lived with a slow, crawling death sentence for so long with Kate, I want what you give me. I find the thought of not having it intolerable."

The fluttering hope closed its wings and took a dive. A rueful smile played on Alida's lips as she regarded the man who was claiming his stake in her future. "So you're hell-bent on having me, no matter what," she said flatly.

"Yes." Totally unequivocal. "I'm thirty-eight years old. You're thirty. Why not make what we can of a life together?"

"It's not much of a basis for marriage."

His hand stroked the curve of her hip. His eyes glinted possessively. "I think it's a hell of a good basis. Better than most."

"God almighty," she breathed, realising that as far as he was concerned, everything hinged on the vital satisfaction she gave him.

Sheer bloody-minded ruthlessness gleamed at her. "You know the consequences, Alida, either way. Take it or leave it."

Choice was a fine thing, but Alida knew in her heart there was only one road to take. She wanted Gareth at her side, not fighting her. "It's not exactly what I've dreamed about," she said with a sigh of resignation.

"Nor I," he acknowledged. "But you'll marry me anyway."

Green eyes mocked his supreme self-assurance. "I might," she said, pride demanding that she never let him know the depth of her feelings for him.

"Why?" he asked. The hand on her hip ceased moving. Again came that intense stillness, the blue eyes probing hers, watching for any response that might give him a further advantage.

Alida let him wait for her answer. She reached out and stroked his cheek. "Because, my dear Gareth, I no longer give a damn," she said softly.

He flinched, then swiftly rolled her onto her back and brushed his lips over hers. "I'll wipe out some of the loneliness in your life, Alida," he murmured. "And I'll be a good father to Andy."

He sealed that pair of promises with a kiss that almost made her forget everything but him and what he could make her feel. Where the road ahead would lead she didn't know, and quite suddenly she didn't care.

Gareth would inevitably give her both pain and pleasure. Where the balance would lie, it was impossible to tell. The future would be what they made of it. That was, of course, if anything could be made of it at all.

"Say yes," he demanded thickly.

"Yes to what?"

His eyes burned into hers. "This is best settled now, Alida. Before I meet Andy."

He was probably right. It didn't matter anyway. "Yes," she said.

"You'll marry me?" Nailing her down.

"Yes."

He kissed her again to take away the pain and make it feel right.

For the moment.

"We'll make arrangements about a wedding with your family this evening," he said, his eyes lit with triumph as he rattled out his plans. "Tomorrow afternoon I have to fly Stacey to Perth for school. I want you and Andy to come with me, Alida. We'll have dinner with my sister and her husband on Sunday night, invite them to the wedding—"

"Aren't you jumping ahead of yourself, Gareth?" Alida cut in with some exasperation at the way he was forging ahead as though he foresaw no difficulties at all. Or meant to override them no matter what. "You haven't even met Andy yet. What if he doesn't take to you?"

"Why shouldn't he? I'm his father," he replied with arrogant simplicity. "It's not as if you've ever said anything to turn him against me."

"Can't you wait and see how he reacts first?"

"Alida, it won't be a problem," he decided. "It's not as if I'm ignorant of how children respond. I like kids. There's nothing for you to worry about there. Flying to Riordan River with us will be a new, exciting adventure to him."

"To . . . to Riordan River?"

"On Monday. I have to get back."

"And you expect us to come with you?"

Her voice shook with the enormity of that step. She simply wasn't mentally or emotionally prepared to take up residence in the home that Gareth had shared with the wife he had loved. It had been different five years ago. She hadn't known about Kate then, not until afterwards. To return to Riordan River, knowing all that she knew now...

"Why not?" Gareth asked, frowning at her. "We'll be married as soon as we can fix a suitable date for everyone. You'll be able to do your designs just as well there as you have here, won't you?"

Alida had no doubt about that. The rugged beauty of Gareth's huge property would be a mine of inspiration. And being with Gareth all the time, living on his cattle station... Surely he would come to see that she could share much more of his life than his bed. Yet she could not control the little shiver of apprehension that ran down her spine at the thought of the homestead being haunted by memories of Kate.

"Alida?" Gareth's frown was deeper, his eyes looking into hers.

The step had to be taken some time if she was marrying Gareth, she argued to herself. "Yes. All right," she answered, and forced a smile. "If everything else goes as you believe it will."

His face relaxed into a confident smile. "Trust me."

At least she would have time to settle in at Riordan River before she had to deal with Kate's daughter there. It was fortunate that Stacey would be at boarding school during the first critical period of this new relationship with Gareth. How the girl would feel, actually seeing Alida in her mother's place... But there was no point in thinking about that problem until she had to meet it. A mad sense of recklessness swept through her mind and brought a gurgle of silly laughter with it.

"There's something amusing about trusting me?" Gareth demanded archly.

"No," she spluttered, looking at the branches where the birds were fluttering to and fro, twittering to each other. "I was wishing it was all much simpler, and I realised how simple you've made it. Like the birds."

"How like the birds?" he queried.

She returned her gaze to his, lightly mocking. "All so basic, Gareth. Mating and seasonal nesting."

The thought sparked amusement and a warm appreciation. "I like your directness."

She breathed a heavy sigh, knowing only too well she had never been completely direct with him. He wasn't the least bit concerned about having her love, but she wanted his. Nevertheless, I can live with compromise, she told herself, as long as I have him.

"Well, we might as well start on this plan of yours," she said dryly. "And see if you can deliver what you think you can."

He laughed and then kissed her again. "I do what has to be done, Alida."

"And accept what cannot be changed," she added.

Their eyes met in a flash of mutual understanding, and Alida felt her heart contract. Perhaps . . . perhaps there was a chance that he would come to love her. Given enough time.

CHAPTER TEN

IT WASN'T UNTIL Gareth's hands were on the steering wheel of the Range Rover and his gaze focused on the track ahead of them that Alida began to reconsider her position. The rough ride to the eastern run jolted second, third and fourth thoughts through her mind.

She had let Gareth seduce her—physically, mentally and emotionally—into accepting *his* plan for the future. Such a decision was hopelessly premature. The least she could have done was make him wait until she was sure a marriage between them was workable. This was a repeat performance of what had happened five years ago. Gareth simply grabbed what he wanted and took it with ruthless disregard for her feelings.

Her eyes shot bitter resentment at him, but the angry feeling got churned into a sick yearning simply by looking at Gareth. There was never going to be any other man for her, she thought with bleak fatalism. But to put her life in his hands, and Andy's as well, those hands on the steering wheel, so sure and strong and resolute, yet capable of such erotic tenderness . . . She shook her head in despair at her desire for him. What about love, she cried inwardly?

"That must be them ahead," Gareth remarked, a lilt of anticipation in his voice.

Alida wrenched her gaze to the windscreen, her heart fluttering in wild agitation as she saw the truck with all the fencing gear. Andy was next to her father at the fence line, pointing toward the Range Rover, alerting his grandpa to its approach.

My son, Alida thought with a fiercely primitive mother love. If Andy didn't take to Gareth, she would change her mind about the marriage. Maybe she would anyhow. It was madness to have allowed him to persuade her into compliance just because of what he could make her feel.

As Gareth slowed the Range Rover to a halt, Andy began running towards them, excitement radiating from his beautiful little face. Alida opened the passenger door and jumped out even before Gareth had turned the ignition off.

"Mummy! Mummy!" Andy piped breathlessly.

She bent down, holding out her arms to him, and Andy hurled himself into them with uninhibited happiness. She swept him up, barely stopping herself from squeezing him too hard as she hugged him to her and swept her mouth over his silky fair hair in a feverish trail of kisses.

"Who's this, Mummy?"

His bright curiosity wrenched at her heart. This is the last moment that Andy is completely mine, Alida thought, then slowly turned to face the inevitability of what was to come.

Gareth was staring at his son, his face softened by a look of half-incredulous wonder that wrenched Alida's heart even more. The words had to be said, and somehow she made herself say them.

"This is your father, Andy."

"My father?" he repeated, not understanding but eager to learn what it meant.

"Your father," Gareth affirmed, a husky note in his voice.

He reached out for his son, and Alida passed over her child to the father he had never known, knowing that their lives were forever changed, knowing that Gareth was not about to give up his plan for the future, knowing that the die was cast beyond recall. A sense of resignation washed over her doubts and fears as she watched what happened between them.

With the simplicity of very young children, Andy readily accepted the man who was claiming him. A few guileless questions, smoothly answered by Gareth, and the matter was unequivocally settled.

Their matching blue eyes gazed upon each other with shining delight, and when Gareth hoisted the excited little boy up to his shoulder in a fatherly hug of possession, Andy reached out and wonderingly touched the cleft in his chin. Gareth placed a finger on the same genetic feature that marked his son, and they laughed together about their likeness, revelling in it, loving it.

So easy, Alida thought with a dark stab of jealousy. Love can be born in a moment. When she had first looked upon Gareth it had been the same, but she had never seen the pure unshadowed light of love he was beaming at his son. With her . . . But there was no point of thinking about that. The decision was made. She could not, would not, deprive Andy of having the relationship that was rightfully his. Only marriage made that possible. And there was no denying that she wanted all she could have of Gareth no matter how much inner anguish came with it.

There were, of course, some reservations from the rest of her family to be overcome, yet Gareth took the meeting with her father and brothers in his stride, as though his presence now was answer enough for all the questions that had never been answered about Andy's father.

He casually announced that he would be marrying Alida as soon as possible. This statement of intention was apparently meant to right any wrong done. Her father and brothers measured him with their eyes as they listened to who he was and where he came from. Alida could see them recognising and approving his likeness to themselves, an Outback man, with all the qualities of character that entailed.

Their decision was written in the respect they subsequently accorded him. Gareth Morgan would do fine for Alida and Andy. They were glad that she at last had a man at her side. It was even better that he was Andy's natural father. As it should be.

Satisfaction all around, Alida thought in dry irony. For men whose life and work revolved around the rules of nature, decisions were shaped by circumstance. She briefly wondered if Gareth would do his best to make their marriage work out right, then decided he would. Whatever *he* considered *best*. Which Alida was yet to find out.

They left her father and brothers to pack up and follow them. Work could be left for such a family occasion as this. The trip to the homestead gave Alida no opportunity to probe Gareth's thoughts about the future. Andy wanted to know everything about his father and peppered him with constant questions.

It was "Daddy, Daddy, Daddy," all the way, and Gareth clearly adored every minute of it, drinking in the reality of the child who was so like himself except for the fair hair he had inherited from Alida. The father and the boy were fascinated and enthralled by each other. Which was understandable, Alida told herself, but she didn't think Gareth's daughter was going to like it.

Stacey was waiting on the veranda for them, standing at the railing beside the front steps. In her jeans and T-shirt, the thin gangliness of early adolescence was only too evident, yet the girl held herself tall and stiff and straight, as though determined to acquit herself well no matter what she felt inside.

She's strong, Alida thought. Her father expected her to accept the situation, and Stacey was not about to let him down. Resolution was stamped on her small expressive face. She might have inherited her mother's features, but it was suddenly clear to Alida that this girl was Gareth's daughter through and through.

Yesterday's confrontation took on another perspective in Alida's mind. Stacey had ruthlessly cut through to what she had perceived as the heart of the matter. As Gareth continually did, but Stacey had not yet learnt adult finesse. Nor had she backed off one inch until Alida had brutally shattered the girl's preconceptions. Even then she had not been quelled from demanding an explanation.

The insight played through Alida's mind as she alighted from the Range Rover. Predictably, Andy chose to follow his father out of the vehicle. He laughed in delight as Gareth swung him to the ground and happily clasped the hand that led him towards his new sister.

Alida saw the shock hit Stacey's face. The girl had not envisaged there being any likeness between her father and a son who had played no part in their lives. Her dark liquid eyes shot a look of vulnerable appeal at Gareth, needing reassurance. Whatever silent message passed between them, the effect on Stacey was instant. She pasted a smile over her shock.

"Is this my big sister, Daddy?" Andy asked, looking at the long-legged girl on the veranda with big-eyed curiosity.

"Yes," said Stacey, and walked down the steps to meet him. She crouched down in front of him, smiling into his face. "Hi, there, Andy. I'm Stacey."

"Stacey," he repeated, giving her a delighted smile in return.

"I guess this is a big surprise for you," she said with friendly appeal.

Andy laughed and looked at Alida, blue eyes shining with happiness. "It's the best big surprise!" Then he turned to Stacey. "Mummy always brings me a surprise when I've been a good boy for Grandma and Grandpa. I was helping Grandpa with the fencing, but I never thought I'd get a father and a sister."

"What did you think you'd get?" Stacey asked.

Andy shook his head. "I don't know. You shouldn't know what surprises are, Stacey," he told her seriously. "It spoils them."

"So it does," she agreed, still smiling as she straightened up. "Your grandma said she was going to make us some drinks." She held out her hand to him. "Will we go and see if they're ready?"

"Yes!" Andy cried, eagerly taking the offered hand and skipping up the steps without a backward glance at Gareth and Alida. "Grandma! Grandma! Guess what Mummy brought me?" he called out excitedly.

Alida watched Stacey take her son inside the house and felt ashamed of her earlier curt rejection of the girl. It had taken enormous character to do what Stacey had done just now. Far from being a spoiled brat, she deserved every consideration Alida could give her. And she would get it in future, Alida silently vowed.

She suddenly became aware that Gareth was watching her. He hadn't moved to follow the children, either. She turned to him with an ironic smile. "You have a fine daughter, Gareth."

"Yes. I'm proud of her," he said quietly. "I also have a fine son, Alida. And I thank you for all you've done to make him so."

"He's mine, too," she said with a hard edge of pride.

"I know." His piercing blue eyes struck deep. "Do we work together or against one another, Alida?"

Straight at the heart, Alida thought. "Together."

His face relaxed into a smile. His eyes caressed her with warm pleasure. It felt so good that Alida could not help smiling at him. And having got what he wanted, Gareth took her hand, threaded his fingers through hers in a clasp of togetherness and drew her with him up the steps to the veranda where the family would inevitably gather.

It was, on the surface of it, a happy family occasion, and it proceeded that way. For the next four hours, both Gareth and Stacey displayed social graces that could not be faulted. They were charming, outgoing, easy company, and not a word out of place was spoken. Alida's family warmed to them as the evening progressed. Dinner turned into a celebratory meal with toasts being drunk to future happiness together.

Alida herself felt oddly detached from the whole scene. It wasn't real, she thought. It was all pretence, hiding a multitude of emotions that Stacey and Gareth and she were studiously covering up. Nevertheless, Alida played her part to the hilt.

She invited Stacey to call her Alida. She assured her mother that all was well, that marriage to Gareth had always been what she wanted although it hadn't been possible until now. She was conscious of her mother watching the interplay between herself and Gareth and Stacey with a much sharper eye than her father and brothers, but she seemed satisfied with the situation.

Andy was first to bed. Stacey excused herself soon afterwards. Alida gave the girl time to settle in her bedroom, then took the opportunity to say a private good-night to her. She knocked on the door. There was no reply. She opened the door a fraction. The bedroom was in darkness.

"Stacey?" she called softly, wondering if the girl had fallen instantly asleep. It had been a long exhausting day with a lot of emotional strain.

Silence for several moments, then a half muffled, "Yes?"

Close to sleep, Alida thought, and decided not to put the light on. "I want to thank you for being so nice to Andy. And to me," she said softly.

A slight gulping sound. "That's okay." The words came out fast, slurred together.

Alida had meant to say more, but the realisation hit her that Stacey was crying. Silently, deeply, forlornly. Her heart twisted with compassion. Yet how could she comfort the girl when she was the person who had ripped Stacey's world apart? Best to leave quickly and get Gareth.

"Good night, Stacey."

"'Night."

Alida closed the door and returned to the dining room where all the adults were still sitting around the table. Her family rarely kept late hours, so she felt no compunction about breaking up the party. "I think I'll call it a night, too," she announced, walking over to Gareth's chair and resting a hand on his shoulder. She stroked it in explicit invitation. Sex was what he wanted from her. If anything would draw Gareth to his feet and come after her, the promise of a repetition of this afternoon's intimacy would surely do it.

He smiled at her, making Alida's stomach curl with the memory of how they had been together. "I'll have to agree with that," he said, clearly thinking of sharing her bed. "It's been a long day."

"That it has," her father chimed in, then bestowed a benevolent smile on both of them. "But a good one."

There was a chorus of good-nights around the table. Alida kissed her mother and father as she always did, then led Gareth into the hallway that took them to the bedroom wing.

The moment they were out of earshot, she said, "Stacey needs you, Gareth."

He stopped her, his eyes sharp and wary. "What do you mean?"

"I mean she needs you to hold her. To tell her you love her. And no matter what else changes, that won't."

Concern creased his brow. "What did she say to you, Alida?"

"Nothing. She was crying when I went to say goodnight. Please go to her, Gareth. Give her the reassurance that she needs. She's held up all day, as you wanted her to, but it wasn't easy for her, Gareth. She's only thirteen, and that's a very uncertain age."

"I know." His mouth twisted an apology. "Thank you for telling me."

He strode off down the hallway without another word, decisive, purposeful, his desire for her instantly put aside for the sake of his daughter whom he loved. He did not so much as glance back as he entered Stacey's bedroom and quietly closed the door behind him.

Alida told herself she was glad he had responded as he had. It showed he had heart. Which she had never really doubted. His love for his wife, his daughter and now his son...

Sex wasn't as important as love. It never would be. And that was what she had committed herself to live with. The lonely emptiness inside her pricked her eyes with tears. Why did it have to be like this, she cried inwardly? But the decision was made, and it was too late to go back on it. She didn't want to anyway. She blinked the tears away, heaved a deep sigh and walked to Andy's bedroom.

There is nothing more beautiful than an innocent little child sleeping peacefully, she thought, gazing lovingly at her son. She gently brushed his silky fair hair off his forehead, then pressed a soft kiss on it, breathing in the clean sweet childish smell of him. Whatever happened with Gareth and Stacey, she would always have Andy to love, and his love in return. At least she had that. And maybe more would come of this marriage. The hope in her heart refused to die.

She washed and went to bed. If Gareth came to her room sometime later, Alida knew nothing of it. Sheer fatigue dragged her quickly into sleep, and when she woke she was still alone. She had forgotten to draw the curtains, and a thin predawn light was coming through her window, but Alida was vaguely conscious that she had been woken by a noise, not the light. She lay still, listening for more sound. Only the familiar bird calls of home broke the silence of early morning. She smiled as she identified them: zebra finches, galahs, honeyeaters.

She pushed the bedclothes aside and padded over to the window in time to see a pair of brilliant green and yellow budgerigars swoop towards the water trough. The air was fresh and the land looked beautiful and mysterious in the soft light, unutterably remote from city life with its traffic noise and business schedules and social pages. Alida felt a singular sense of relaxation as she watched a spotted bowerbird hopping along the ground, pecking for insects. Real needs were very simple far from the centres of civilisation.

The whinny of a horse drew her attention to the stable yards beyond the barn. The thought of an early morning ride before anyone else was up was attractive. The idea had no sooner drifted through her mind than she saw Stacey leading a saddled horse to the stable yard gate. The girl was clearly intent on going out for a ride by herself.

Alida frowned. As confident as Stacey might be in looking after herself, this was not familiar country to her. If she went too far, did she have the tracking knowledge to find her way back? Alida hesitated only a moment before turning to the wardrobe to get out her riding gear. Her company might not be welcomed, but it was better to be safe than sorry. Besides, it was a chance to speak to the girl and perhaps establish some understanding between them.

By the time Alida set out after Stacey, the girl and her horse were only a spurt of dust in the distance. Alida followed as swiftly as common sense and the inclination of her horse allowed. She enjoyed the canter. She hoped that Stacey would see that they actually had a lot in common, and that Alida could and would fit into her life and Gareth's. She had to. For Andy's sake, if not for her own.

It was one of those ironies of life that Stacey should choose as her destination the same waterhole where her father had persuaded Alida to marry him. Alida dismounted and tethered her own to a nearby tree, then followed the girl's footsteps across the dry creek bed to the other side of the waterhole. She found a pair of riding boots and socks placed neatly together at the base of the rock climb that she and her brothers had attempted and failed so many times.

"Stacey?" she called, hoping the girl had not climbed her way into trouble.

"I'm up here." There was a slight quaver in her voice.

"Are you okay?"

Silence.

Alida couldn't see her, but the sound of her voice had come from the split chasm above the waterhole, and that section was definitely dangerous. Alida went to the horses and removed the bridles and reins. They would do for a makeshift rope if one was needed to haul Stacey to safety.

"Alida?" There was a touch of panic in that cry. Pride giving way to fear.

"I'm coming," Alida yelled as she ran across the creek bed.

"I . . . I need help."

"Hold on as best you can, Stacey. I'll get to you as fast as I can make it." She hung the reins around her neck and swiftly removed her own riding boots and socks.

"The ledge crumbled under my foot and...and I'm not sure I should move."

"Don't move. Just hold on and wait."

With the expert knowledge of many previous climbs, Alida started up the easiest rock buttress.

"Alida?"

"I'm on my way."

"Maybe . . . maybe you should get Dad."

A vote of no-confidence, Alida thought grimly. The problem was that Stacey might not be able to hang on that long. Toes could cramp. She might be tempted to move and get herself into a worse jam.

"Stacey, I've lived here all my life," she reminded the girl. "I'm older than my brothers. I used to get them out of their scrapes. Some of them involved this rock face, which I know as well as the palm of my hand. You might think of me as a soft city person, but before I was sent to boarding school in Perth, one of my jobs was to lead out a team of Aboriginal stockmen on muster. I was in the saddle for twelve hours at a time, and camped with the men for up to six weeks bringing the stock in. So please, give me a little credit for knowing what I'm doing, will you?"

Silence.

Alida hoped it meant Stacey was digesting that information. "I wasn't meaning to brag. That was just the way it was," she said matter-of-factly, hoping to keep Stacey's mind occupied until she could reach her. "My mum and dad couldn't afford permanent help, so I filled in wherever I was needed. I guess you've helped your father on his station, too."

A pause, then, "Did you hate being sent away to school?" Stacey's voice was less of a quaver now, more filled with curiosity.

"Yes. It felt like being put in jail. And all the other girls seemed to know more than I did about everything. But it was what my parents wanted for me, and it was costing them so much to give me a proper education that I knew I had to do the best I could. I got used to it after a while, but I was always glad to get home.''

A longer pause.

Alida quickened her progress as much as she could, but the footholds were tricky with loosened shale and she had to feel her way carefully in some places.

''My mother used to teach me,'' Stacey said in a forlorn little voice.

Alida didn't know what reply to make. Stacey's mother was a touchy subject. The girl didn't want Alida trying to take her place. Heaven alone knew what Stacey thought about Andy's conception while her mother was still alive! How had Gareth explained that?

''I guess you miss your mother very much,'' she offered sympathetically.

A choking sound.

Alida's heart sank. The last thing she needed was Stacey being emotional. She tried to force the girl's mind onto something else.

''I think you ought to get your plaits cut off,'' she said. ''With your small face you'd look much prettier with short hair.''

The sniffing stopped. ''My mother liked my hair long. She used to brush it every day,'' came the angry protest.

''Well, she's not here to brush it any more. And I bet it's a nuisance to you at boarding school,'' Alida suggested. The appeal to vanity didn't seem to be working.

"It is not. I can keep it just like my mother did."

"It's *your* hair, Stacey."

"You're only saying that because..."

Silence.

"Because what?" Alida prompted.

"Because you hated my mother!"

So the terrible truth was out. Alida took a deep breath and produced a flat matter-of-fact voice. "You can't hate someone you don't know, Stacey. I never knew your mother. I couldn't hate her."

"You did so hate her. When you spoke about her in the car you hated her."

"Not her, Stacey. I hated the position I was in. I never meant to be the other woman in anybody's marriage. If I'd hated your mother, I could have hurt her by telling her about Andy. I could have written her a letter. Or sent her a photograph. But I didn't do it. I never did anything to stop your parents from being happy together."

She reached the cut in the rock face and edged around it. Stacey was clinging to a fissure on the next giant step up and about two metres along from Alida's position. Her feet were hanging onto a ledge that had broken away on either side of her. A tear-streaked face peered down at Alida, but the dark eyes were clear of any distorting moisture.

The incline was such that they could both lean against the rock face, which gave them some security against falling headlong down the chasm. Alida judged that with the reins looped under Stacey's arms, the girl could slide down to Alida's level and be steadied there.

She set about making the necessary loops as she calmly explained to Stacey what she wanted her to do. It was a tricky manouvre that required both nerve and steady caution. The girl looked frightened but she didn't lose her head and panic. She followed Alida's instructions step by step. When Stacey had as firm a grip as she could get on the fissure, Alida braced herself to take the weight should the girl fumble the foothold on the lower level.

"Okay. Press yourself against the rock. Take one foot off the ledge and steady yourself before taking the other off. Then let go slowly and slide."

There were a few teetering moments before she landed on the lower ledge, but Alida had the reins pulled tight in a flash, slamming her forward against the incline. She was safe. Yet in the next instant there was a shower of stone from where she had hung onto the fissure, and although it would have been quite harmless, Stacey panicked into moving away from it. She lunged towards Alida, accidentally unbalancing her.

Even as Alida began to fall, it spun through her mind that she had to let go the reins. She opened her hands and the leather straps slid away from her. Stacey's scream rang in her ears, but there was nothing Alida could do to save herself. She was falling the wrong way—outwards—and the last thing she thought of was to let herself go limp. Then her head hit against rock and she knew nothing more.

How long it was before she became conscious again, Alida had no idea. Time was meaningless. She gradually became aware of pain. It felt as though her head was splitting. There was whirling darkness. Movement. Noise. She forced her eyes open. At least she thought she did, but still there was only whirling darkness.

"Alida."

Gareth's voice, urgent, harsh with concern.

The pain in her head was excruciating as she turned it towards his voice.

"Thank God!" he breathed. "Alida, try to move your legs."

She did. A little. She seemed to hurt all over.

"That's fine," Gareth said in a shaky relief. "Lie still now. We're almost back at the homestead."

"Gareth, I can't see," Alida forced out, her voice sounding thick and faraway.

"There's nothing important to see, Alida," he soothed. "Some bruising. A few cuts and grazes that will soon heal. No bones broken that I can detect. Just lie still and don't worry about anything. Stacey's okay. She climbed down and rode back to us for help. And you're going to be okay, too."

But her eyes were open. She was sure they were. So why couldn't she see something besides whirling darkness? The vehicle she was in? Gareth? He was beside her, wasn't he?

"I can't see," she said again, a welling of panic heightening the pain.

"Open your eyes."

"They are open. Aren't they?"

She heard his sharply indrawn breath. Then in a strained voice, "It must be concussion. Close your eyes and rest, Alida. Don't worry about it. We'll get you to a hospital as fast as we can."

People got dizzy from concussion. She knew that. But surely they didn't lose their sight altogether. That didn't seem right at all. Yet if it wasn't right, then she had somehow gone blind.

Please God, don't let it be so, she prayed in desperate anguish. Let it be only temporary. She couldn't be blind. Not from such a simple accident. Not when she was going to marry Gareth. Not when she had saved Stacey. Please, God, don't let it be so.

CHAPTER ELEVEN

THE LAST WEEK before the bandages came off was the hardest for Alida. As much as she told herself she should be abrim with anticipation for the moment she saw light again, she could not quell the fear of that moment never coming. What if the surgeon was wrong? What if the operation hadn't been a success? What if she stayed blind forever?

The long days of darkness seemed interminable. The loss of sight made her feel helpless, disoriented, claustrophobic, totally cut off from the world she had always taken for granted. Whenever she was alone, a crazy panic about the future would creep up on her and overwhelm all the common sense she tried to apply.

Gareth seemed to take it for granted that nothing would go wrong as far as her eyes were concerned. The damage caused by internal haemorrhaging had been repaired and it was only a matter of time before she had her sight back. All the arrangements of the wedding were made. The waiting was almost over. There was a deep impatient hunger in his kisses that stirred an equal hunger in Alida, a desperate hunger for everything to turn out right for them.

In some ways the accident and her temporary blindness had not been a bad thing. These past weeks in the hospital and then this nursing home had given her much more assurance that her marriage to Gareth was not such a terrible gamble. He had stayed on in Perth to be with her and Andy, making sure she got the best treatment, keeping her company, meeting her city friends and getting to know them.

He liked Jill Masters. She could tell from the easy rapport between them. He was neutral about Suzanne Day, polite to her but nothing more. Ivan Poletti he was slower to accept. If Alida didn't know better, she would have thought Gareth was jealous of their friendship. But that was ridiculous. And gradually she heard amusement in Gareth's voice when he spoke of him or to him.

It also relieved Alida's mind that Gareth never said anything negative about her career although she knew he didn't like it. The idea of giving it up and living full-time with Gareth was very tempting. Somehow dress designing held no compelling interest for her anymore. It had always been a substitute for what she really wanted. Yet reason insisted that it was wiser to keep on with it and retain some independence.

If she couldn't have Gareth's love, she might very well need a breathing space away from him, something to pour herself into and forget what she didn't have. Besides, wasn't it said that absence made the heart grow fonder? Perhaps it would sharpen Gareth's desire for her after each separation, and keep that spice in their marriage for him.

Sometimes when he sat with her at night and softly stroked her hand and arm, she let herself imagine he really loved her. Gareth was such a strange mixture of hardness and gentleness. The ruthless savage she had called him in her mind was not so much in evidence these days.

To her surprise and intense pleasure, he had presented her with an engagement ring, an emerald surrounded by a flowing wave of baguette diamonds. It wasn't a bond of love. She knew that. Gareth had spelled out what it meant.

"I know I haven't done much right by you, Alida, but I hope this will make up for some of the hurt I've given you. It's a token of my esteem for you, and a symbol of my commitment to our marriage."

It made Alida feel that he did care for her, above and beyond sexual attraction. Although a little worm of cynicism whispered that the gesture was probably more aimed to ensure that she didn't change her mind about marrying him.

That was why he stayed on in Perth with her. "Don't you have to get back to Riordan River, Gareth?" she had asked in the early days after the operation on her eyes.

"I'm not going until I can take you with me, Alida," he had replied, firm resolution in his voice.

That had been his plan before the accident, to take her and Andy straight to Riordan River with him.

Gareth was taking no chances that their marriage agreement would break down anywhere along the way. Yet she had no intention of changing her mind. Andy adored his father. Stacey showed every sign of accepting her. Alida sensed there was an underlying guilt in all the girl's visits to her, but at least there was no sign of hostility.

Stacey seemed endlessly curious about the facts of life, and they had several frank discussions on the subject. Not exactly mother talk, Alida thought ruefully, but Stacey obviously didn't want another mother. Perhaps she had decided that stepmothers were something quite different.

Deborah Hargreaves' easy acceptance of the situation was another bonus as far as Alida was concerned. Not only did Gareth's sister insist on organizing the wedding for them, but she warmly extended her friendship to Alida, often coming to visit her in the morning, armed with cryptic crossword puzzles that she said Alida could help her with.

In actual fact, the accident had been quite fortuitous in settling a number of potential problems. The way their marriage would work now had more reassuring substance to it with the sorting out of other relationships. As well, Alida no longer felt quite so threatened by the memory of Kate Morgan. She felt more confident of handling whatever came, once she regained her sight.

The day of the unveiling finally arrived. Alida did her best to hide her inner tension. Gareth was beside her, chatting to the eye specialist and his associate as the bandages were removed. No-one seemed to nurse any doubt that the operation could have been anything but a complete success. The pads from her eyelids were gently lifted away, the last constriction to her seeing again.

"Now open your eyes," the specialist instructed.

She did.

But there was no light.

"I can't..." she started, then choked on the panic welling up in her.

"Patience, Miss Rose. It will take a few moments for your eyes to become acclimatised to light again."

The few moments stretched into many more with no result. Please, please, Alida prayed wildly, desperately. This couldn't happen to her. Hadn't she suffered enough? Where was the reward for all the pain? She was going to marry Gareth tomorrow. She *needed* to see.

But her prayers weren't answered.

"No. There's nothing," she forced out after an aeon of anguished waiting. "No light. Nothing but the same...the same darkness."

And then began the darkest hour of all, the agonisingly slow examination, eyes right, eyes left, look up, look down, stare straight ahead. The humming and hawing. A slower recovery than expected. Perhaps in more time. These things took time.

The specialist and his associate kept on talking to each other. They talked to Gareth, who was asking questions. Alida stopped listening. What they said didn't matter any more.

She was blind. And no one knew when, if ever, her sight would come back. That was what Alida had to face. And it changed the darkness to the blackest of black despairs because nothing could ever be truly right now. Her mind ticked relentlessly over the stark truths that jagged through her churning emotions.

Marriage to Gareth was unthinkable. To be a handicapped wife, like Kate, totally dependent on Gareth. Alida couldn't do it. He didn't love her as he had loved Stacey's mother. The future ahead of them was not the future either of them had had in mind when their marriage was agreed upon. She had to release Gareth from his commitment to her, cancel the wedding.

And then what?

Her career as a designer was finished. She couldn't see to sketch anything. Or to choose colour. Was she never to see colour again? Merciful heaven! What was to become of her? A whole future of this dreadful darkness?

Alida fought down the sickening panic. She couldn't afford to dissolve into a quivering mess. There were things she had to do and say. Pride insisted that Gareth be shown she was capable of standing on her own, no matter what. Somehow she would reshape her life and make something out of it when she learned to cope with this terrifying disability.

The specialist and his associate took their leave of her, mouthing their optimistic platitudes. Alida thanked them. Undoubtedly they had done their best for her. It wasn't their fault she was blind.

She heard the door open and shut as Gareth ushered them out of her room. He came back, crouched down beside her, took her hands in his, gently rubbed them. He inhaled a deep breath, then slowly released it.

"Alida," he said quietly, "I know this must be a crushing disappointment for you."

"Don't go on, Gareth." She couldn't bear it. She knew what she had to do and it was best done now. She forced a calm decisive tone into her voice. "I appreciate very much, all your kindness and consideration. The way you've taken care of everything for me since the accident—"

"Alida..."

"No!" She drew a hand from his gentle grasp and lifted it to where his face had to be. Her fingers fumbled over his lips. "Please listen to me."

"Whatever you want," he said huskily.

She swallowed hard. Her mind dictated the words and her mouth delivered them as ordered. "I can't marry you, Gareth. So all this, all you've been doing has to stop. You can still be a father to Andy. Perhaps it's best if you have him most of the time. At least until I learn to manage."

"No." An explosive negative.

She lost touch with him. He must be shaking his head, Alida thought. His fingers gripped her hand more tightly.

"We're getting married. You gave me your word, Alida. The wedding is all arranged for tomorrow. We are getting married," he repeated with hard decisiveness.

"You can't want it. I won't do it," she cried in protest.

"Why not?" he demanded.

"Because it's wrong."

"In what way?"

Why was he making this so difficult for her? Why was he hammering at her like this? He couldn't possibly want to be married to her now. He could only be insisting out of some stupid sense of honour. Dear God! She knew all about internal haemorrhaging. Her heart was bleeding as she forced herself to deny him for his own sake. Every word was killing her.

"You know I can't be the kind of wife you should have, Gareth. You've already been through one marriage with a handicapped woman. You understand all the stress it involved. To load yourself down with a blind—"

"You won't stay blind, Alida," he argued fiercely.

"What if I do?"

"Then we adjust to it. There are many people without their sight who lead full lives—"

"Gareth, do you hear what I'm saying?" she cut in desperately. "You don't *need* me. You can have Andy.

I'll only be a burden to you. I've never been a burden to anyone before. I don't want that. I'd hate it.''

"I *want* to take care of you, Alida." His voice vibrated with deep passion.

"That's guilt talking, Gareth. You think you have to do right by me. Because of Stacey and Andy, and maybe because of what happened in the past. That's part of why you gave me this ring.''

She slipped her hands from his and started to tug off his token of commitment.

"No!" His fingers crushed hers, making removal of the emerald ring impossible. "What the hell kind of man do you think I am, Alida?" he rasped. "I don't turn my back on adversity.''

"I know. But that's not the point,'' she cried plaintively.

"What is the point?''

"My being blind. It was an accident. Simply an accident. You don't have to pay for it. And I won't let you.''

"Alida, what I do is my choice. Not yours.''

"I know how you feel. Can't you understand that?'' she pleaded. "You said you didn't want to live the rest of your life with guilt. You said—''

"Whatever I said doesn't apply to this situation,'' he insisted, his voice beating at her from above as he straightened.

"You have to see...''

He grasped her other hand and pulled her out of the chair, enfolding her in a tight embrace. "I want you,'' he said thickly. "That's what I see. That's what I know. That's what I understand. I want you, Alida. And every day that passes, I want you more."

He swept warm soft kisses around her temples, closed her eyes with kisses. Alida stood helpless in his embrace, trembling with the warring forces of her need for him and the despair of having to reject that need.

Gareth lifted her hands to his shoulders. She slid them down, meaning to press away from him. Her fingers instinctively lingered over the strong muscles so clearly defined under the thin fabric of his shirt. Her palm came to rest over his heart, and it was as though the quick heavy beat swept into her bloodstream, bonding her life force to his.

"Gareth." His name was whispered from her lips in a moan of tortured longing. "You must let me go."

His mouth covered hers, rendering such words powerless with a sweet, seductive sensuality that Alida found impossible to fight. It was entrancing in its tenderness, as though Gareth felt more than desire for her. Compassion, perhaps.

She shouldn't have responded, yet somehow she couldn't help herself, and the soft movement of her lips under his was quickly possessed by Gareth who used every tantalising incitement to draw her with him into the wild passion that drowned out everything else. He sapped her will with a deep, enervating persuasion that demanded she acknowledge one reality—him—and his desire for her, no matter how wrong it was.

As his mouth took hers into a drowning well of sensation, his hands made love to her, moulding her body to the desire coursing through his, allowing her no respite from the yearning within, feeding it with his touch, with the feel of him wanting her, needing her.

When he started to undress her, Alida had a pang of awareness of where they were. "You can't!" she moaned. "Anyone could come in."

"Damn them all!" he muttered. "I put a Don't Disturb sign on the door."

His mouth burned a trail of kisses down her throat, choking off any further speech. The intensity of his desire for her pulsed through Alida in melting waves. Forced by her blindness into an inner world of feeling, everything seemed more intense. She could not see the expression on Gareth's face, could not see what was reflected in his eyes, but what emanated from his mouth and hands and body was an overwhelming hunger for all of her.

He undressed her slowly, seemingly intent on savouring to the full every part of her feminity. He kissed and caressed her as though luxuriating in the feel of her skin, the taste of her flesh, as though he couldn't bear not to know, not to experience everything about her, and she had the sense of him feasting on the tremors of pleasure that rippled through her body under the enthralling excitement of his touch.

He lifted her onto the bed. She heard the discarding of his clothes and quivered in anticipation for what was to follow. I'll have this to remember, she thought, excusing the weakness that craved this last time with him.

His fingertips feathered over the soles of her feet, trailed exquisitely up the calves of her legs, stroked her inner thighs. The bed was depressed under his weight. She reached for him, but he eluded the embrace she offered. She felt the warmth of his breath on her thighs, experienced a shock of incredible sensation as his mouth grazed over the most intimate part of her, delicately caressing in the sweetest of all tortures.

"Gareth." His name scraped from her throat in a grown of ecstatic despair. If only he could be hers forever. If only this could go on for eternity. If only they had met and loved in some other life where nothing came between them, as nothing did now.

He slid his body up over hers and she hugged him tightly to her, so tightly she felt the strained tautness of his muscles. His flesh was warm and strong and sleekly beautiful. She wanted to melt into him. She found his mouth and kissed him with all the primitive fervour in her soul and heart and body.

He lifted her to meet the power of his need and she welcomed the full thrust of him inside her, revelling in the sense of belonging together, sighing with the wondrous fulfilment of having him sharing an inner world that needed no vision.

He stayed still for several piercingly sweet moments, as though he, too, was savouring the feeling of completeness with her. "Alida," he breathed, and to her ears it sounded like a reverberating echo of her own glorious satisfaction.

He moved slowly at first, as though entranced by every minute sensation. She heard the quivering catch in his breath each time he drew back to plunge again, deeper and deeper as she opened for him and closed around him.

"Alida." Husky emotion, something beyond want and need like disbelieving wonder.

She let her hands and body speak their language of love, knowing that she could not say any words. The freedom of her response to him was the gift of her love, unleashed from the chains of a reality that made any future together impossible. For this time—this precious hour—the only reality was the blissful fusion of his body with hers.

Alida didn't want to think. She clung to the mindless sense of simply being with Gareth until he stirred and spoke. "No more talk of not marrying me, Alida," he said, his voice throbbing with determined conviction. "You *will* marry me!" She could feel the strong vibration of it in his throat where he held her head tucked under his chin. "Whatever happens about your sight, it changes nothing for me. Whatever you are, you're the woman I want. I've never felt less burdened than I do at this moment with you."

He rolled her onto the pillows and kissed her mouth, imparting his contentment with soft dreamy pleasure. Alida thought about what he said, slowly coming to the realisation that the basis for which Gareth wanted their marriage had not changed. Her blindness did not stop her from functioning as a woman. In that way she was not handicapped at all. Most married couples made love in the dark.

Would it be terribly weak of her to give in and accept what he offered? She wanted him so much. Always had. Always would. Losing her career was nothing if she could have him.

If Gareth was satisfied with her sharing his bed, perhaps their marriage was workable, despite her inability to share other aspects of his life. And since those other aspects were familiar to her, she would be able to talk about them with him.

Her career couldn't separate her from him now. Perhaps with Gareth that would be a plus. She would be a full-time wife at Riordan River, which gave rise to a number of very positive thoughts about the future. If Gareth didn't mind her blindness.

She reached up and touched his face. The muscles around his jawline relaxed. She felt his head turn, and he kissed her fingertips. His pleasure in her brought a tremulous smile of pleasure to her lips.

"You'll marry me tomorrow," he said as though it was definitely decided. "As promised."

Her smile faded as she inwardly looked at the difficulties ahead. "I may not be an easy person to live with," she warned tentatively. "I'm not used to being dependent."

"You won't be dependent for long. I know you better than you think, Alida. You'll be managing your own life again in very short time," he said dryly.

"I haven't been doing that lately," she reminded him.

"That's because you were waiting. Waiting is worse than anything else. It renders everyone powerless, helpless..."

There was a sad, heavy note in his voice. Was he thinking of Kate, Alida wondered? Remembering how there had been no happy ending for all the waiting, remembering how helpless he had been to change what couldn't be changed. Would Riordan River be haunted by Kate? Even more haunted because Alida also would be a handicapped wife?

Gareth sighed then struck a more cheerful, positive note. "We can move forward now."

"If it doesn't work out, Gareth—"

"We'll work it out, Alida," he insisted firmly. "You think I haven't seen you're as strong-minded as I am? We can work through anything together. I have no doubt of it."

Hope swirled over her fears. To be always together with Gareth... But emotions could defeat the strongest minds and spirits. "What about Stacey?" she asked.

"You're already good for Stacey. She talks to you and listens to you."

"She'll feel so guilty that I'm blind."

Gareth ignored that claim. "It will be good for Andy, as well. Having both parents together is a definite plus."

Alida sighed at his relentless persistence. "You won't take no for an answer, will you?"

"No. I won't."

"I don't know, Gareth," she said in agonised uncertainty. "I don't want you to ever feel stuck with me. Promise me if you ever begin to feel that..."

"Alida, trust me. I know what I'm doing. I know what I want. Let it be, Alida."

Trust. It came with love, didn't it? A deep abiding love. It was what she felt for Gareth. And she didn't believe he would ever betray her trust if she gave it. He hadn't betrayed Kate's trust. He wanted to marry her, and if she was the woman he wanted more than any other woman...

"Stop worrying," he commanded. "Tomorrow we start our life together. And I promise you, you will never be a burden to me."

She wished she could see his eyes. He was asking for a blind act of faith in him. All the love in her heart urged her to put doubts aside, to believe what he told her, because this was the man her heart had chosen. It was right to trust him. It had to be.

"Yes, tomorrow," she whispered, too choked with emotion to find more voice.

He heard the surrender in her barely audible murmur and kissed her again to seal the trust between them.

CHAPTER TWELVE

THIS IS MY WEDDING DAY and I don't know what I look like, Alida thought as her mother arranged a coronet of flowers on her hair. She was sitting in front of her dressing table in her home at Claremont, but only her mother could see the reflection in the mirror. Tears pricked Alida's eyes. She fought them back. She wouldn't cry. Not for any reason.

Today was to be a happy day. The tears had all been shed yesterday. What couldn't be changed had to be accepted. She was lucky, she told herself fiercely, terribly lucky to have the man she loved wanting her to be his wife.

"A really good guy," as Jill had gruffly proclaimed last night. And she was lucky to have a friend like Jill, who had insisted she was not to worry about business matters, to leave everything in her capable hands. And Ivan fussing over her this morning, describing the way Jonathon was doing her hair, declaring that he had always wanted to visit an Outback station and she was to invite him whenever she wanted some truly interesting company. She also had all her family with her, giving their loving support on this fateful day.

"Is your headache gone?" her mother asked, concern threading her voice.

"Yes," Alida lied, not wanting her mother worried by it.

The pain behind her eyes was dulled at the moment, but she doubted anything was going to banish it today, no matter how many pills she took. Tension had been building up in her ever since she had given in to Gareth's persuasion yesterday. Then the stress of trying to think of business with Jill last night. She had gone to bed with an excruciating headache, hoping to lose it in sleep, but she had woken with it this morning. Perhaps it would go away when the deed was done and the marriage certificate signed, Alida thought fatalistically.

Her mother declared that the coronet of flowers made her look precisely as a bride should look, softly feminine and very beautiful. At least Alida could smell the flowers. Stephanotis, her mother said. Very popular for bridal bouquets. A sprinkling of lemon and white daisies as well. She had felt them. They would look right with her clothes.

She knew what she was wearing. The creamy lemon two-piece was one of her most feminine designs. The top had organza inserts beaded in daisy patterns, and the full circular skirt was the perfect complement to it. Not exactly a wedding dress, she thought ruefully, but the idea of a real wedding dress hadn't felt right.

Besides, today she was really saying goodbye to her own world, as well as the world of fashion design. It seemed fitting to wear something reflecting what she had done with her life up until now. What the future held for her, apart from being with Gareth, she didn't know. In an hour or two she would place her hand in his, and he would lead her to whatever would be. She desperately hoped she wasn't doing the wrong thing in marrying him.

What was Stacey feeling today?

"There," her mother said with satisfaction, lifting her hands away from the flowers positioned in Alida's hair.

Alida could hear the smile in her voice, so she smiled, too. The bride was supposed to smile at her wedding. Just as winners were supposed to smile at award presentations. She wondered if she would ever have met Gareth again if he had not been there that night at the award presentations. It had been such a coincidence. If he had not turned up... But she wouldn't think about that. So much had changed since then. But the biggest change would undoubtedly come when Gareth took her home with him to Riordan River.

"We're all ready now," her mother declared cheerfully. "Let me show you off to your father."

Alida kept her smile in place as her mother led her out to the living room where the rest of her family were gathered waiting for her. They declared she looked beautiful, but there was a catch of emotion in their voices that was almost Alida's undoing. She had to swallow hard to keep her composure. It wasn't easy being blindly beautiful to her father and brothers.

Andy saved the moment, demanding that she bend down so he could smell the flowers in her hair. Then her mother announced that the car had arrived for them, and the ensuing activity was gratefully seized upon by everyone. Gareth had sent a white stretch limousine, which comfortably seated the six of them.

"I must say your husband-to-be does things in style, Alida," one of her brothers commented appreciatively.

"He's a good man," her father approved.

"He's very good with Andy, too," her mother chimed in.

"Daddy says we're flying to his home tomorrow," Andy informed them all. "It's real big like your place, Grandpa."

The talk moved to station life, and Alida let her mind drift to memories of home. She wondered how long it would take before Riordan River felt like home to her, if it ever would, if she could carve out her own place there, something completely separate from what Kate Morgan had established. She wished she could forget about Gareth's first marriage.

What was Gareth feeling? Was he really sure he would always want her? Was he having second thoughts about his decision to marry her? Alida determinedly pushed such ideas away. They sharpened the pain in her head. Gareth had asked her to trust him. She did. She had to.

They arrived at Deborah's home at Peppermint Grove. Both Gareth and Stacey were on hand to greet them. Alida's pulse raced with nervous tension. Her father helped her out of the limousine then passed her to Gareth, warm hands enfolding her cold ones.

She looked up automatically, fiercely wishing she could see his face and read what he was thinking. She was totally unaware of her own piercingly vulnerable expression.

"The sun is shining, just as it should for you," Gareth said huskily. "You outshine the sun, Alida."

Her heart turned over at the feeling in his voice. He still wanted her. Her trust in him was not misplaced.

"Alida, could you turn your head a bit and smile?" Stacey pleaded. "I want to take some photographs to show the girls at school. Put your arm around her, Dad."

There was an excited lilt in Stacey's voice. Gareth's arm hugged Alida to his side. Her smile wobbled between relief and pleasure at the thought that Stacey might actually welcome her as a stepmother.

There were several clicks, then Stacey's voice again, warm and admiring. "That's fine! You look absolutely beautiful, Alida."

"I'm glad you think so, Stacey," Alida replied, hope surging through her other turbulent emotions.

She heard a couple of quick steps. A soft kiss was pressed onto her cheek. "I'm glad you're marrying Dad. I hope you don't mind getting me, too," Stacey whispered.

Surprised and momentarily nonplussed, Alida reached out and managed to catch the girl's arm. "I want ... I hope we can be friends, if that's all right."

"That's great by me," Stacey assured her.

The sincere fervour in her voice sounded marvellous to Alida. Had Gareth been right about her being good for his daughter?

"Hey, Andy!" Stacey called out. "Come over here and get your photo taken with your mum and dad. Mr. Rose, will you take a shot of the four of us together?"

"Do my best," he cheerfully agreed.

"Aunty Deb bought me a lemon dress so we'd look neat together," Stacey informed Alida. "And I got my hair cut and styled. I took Mr. Poletti's advice and went to Jonathan Lee. All the girls at school are green with envy. Here, feel."

She picked up Alida's hand and lifted it to her hair, which was cut very short. Was this some act of penance, Alida worried? Was the girl putting on a bright act to make up for what had happened? Or was the haircut a statement that everything was going to be different from now on?

"I'm a thoroughly modern girl, aren't I, Dad?"

"She's added about three years to her age and looks far too pretty for her own good," Gareth said dryly.

Stacey giggled. It sounded like a happy giggle. As though she had put the past behind her and was beginning to enjoy the present. As for the future, it was looking more hopeful to Alida by the second. At least where Stacey was concerned.

Gareth guided her inside his sister's house. Alida had the feeling of spaciousness around her. The carpet underfoot was thick and soft. Of course, it would be a very luxurious home, she surmised, and hoped Gareth would stop her from tripping over anything or knocking something precious over. She hugged his arm tightly, swept by a nervous sense of insecurity.

"Trust me to look after you, Alida," he murmured. "I won't let anything go wrong."

The complete assurance in his voice settled some of the flutters in her stomach. Deborah greeted her in a subtle cloud of Anais Anais, then introduced her husband, Max, whose handshake was firm and friendly. He had a deep crisp voice. Alida imagined he would be incisive in boardroom meetings.

Their two sons were introduced, both bright and friendly boys. They took Andy off to show him some new toys. New cousins, Alida thought. And a new aunt and uncle. Andy's world was widening in leaps and bounds. Alida could hear the breathless excitement in his voice.

Dear God! Please let his work out right, she prayed fervently. *If I have to be blind, then help me make this marriage a success. Let us all be happy together.*

Max poured a round of champagne for the adults. Alida only took a few token sips from her glass, wary of making her headache worse.

The celebrant arrived. Deborah ushered them into a room that was heavily scented with roses. Alida heard Stacey's camera click several times as they took their positions for the ceremony.

This is it, she thought, the moment I've yearned for and thought would never be mine, to be married to the man I want with me for the rest of my life. I'll be a good wife to him, she silently vowed. I'll make him glad he chose to marry me, even though I am blind. Kate could not have loved him more than I will. And I won't be a burden. I'll learn not to be. I'll learn so fast, he'll hardly know I'm blind at all.

She was barely aware of what the celebrant said as he read out the marriage service. He was a stranger, performing a job he was being paid to do. It meant nothing special to him. The real ceremony was in her heart and soul.

She spoke the words when she was directed to. She heard Gareth speak them, too, enunciating the promises in a firm strong voice, and she wondered what he felt in his heart and soul. They were binding words, but they meant little if he did not feel the same bond she felt. How long did passionate desire last?

Gareth took her left hand and slid the symbol of marriage onto her finger. "With this ring, I thee wed."

His voice was still firm and strong and purposeful. No retreat from Gareth Morgan. Not the slightest wavering. He had made his decision. This was his commitment. Now for the follow-through.

"You may kiss the bride."

Gareth drew her into a gentle embrace. Alida sensed the tight restraint in him as he kissed her with tenderness. She knew instinctively that if others had not been watching he would have kissed her very differently. She did not need to see him to feel his desire reaching out, wanting to envelop her. Excitement tingled along her nerves at the brushing of his body against hers.

Their family surrounded them, breaking up any privacy with hugging, shaking hands, kissing, offering congratulations and best wishes for future happiness together. An atmosphere of celebratory pleasure swirled around Alida. She felt welcomed into Gareth's family and proudly loved by her own. Somehow her blindness didn't seem to matter so much.

Max thrust a glass of champagne into her hand. Toasts were drunk. Music was played. Alida did her best to ignore the headache that was growing steadily worse. Signing the marriage certificate hadn't worked any magic on it at all. She tried to keep smiling and looking happy, but the pain was making it more and more difficult.

It was a relief when Max informed her that Suzanne Day had come to see her on urgent business and was in the library waiting on Alida's convenience. It would be quiet in the library, Alida thought. She would ask Gareth to get her some pain-killers while she talked to Suzanne.

Alida couldn't imagine what emergency had drawn Suzanne here. Jill had promised to handle all business matters, and Jill Masters was nothing if not efficient. Apart from which, all her friends had been told that her wedding to Gareth would be a strictly family affair, no other guests. There had to be a dire emergency. One that Jill couldn't advise on.

No sooner were they inside the room than Suzanne broke into a babble of nervous apologies for intruding.

"What is the problem?" Gareth asked, cutting straight to the heart of the matter.

"The operation on Alida's eyes wasn't a success," Suzanne blurted out baldly.

"Not as yet," Gareth bit out, an edge of anger in his voice.

"If she's blind, she can't design."

Alida could feel her face tightening under the blunt impact of those words. "*I am here,* Suzanne. I might be blind, but I can hear as well as anyone. Please give me the courtesy of telling me whatever problem you have. Gareth has no knowledge of my business."

"I'm sorry, Alida," Suzanne rushed out in obvious distress. "This is all a dreadful shock. It didn't hit me until an hour ago that you've got both me and my factory under contract. Until the end of next season. But there isn't going to be any next season's designs from you, is there? So before you fly off somewhere, doing whatever you're going to do, I need you to sign a release of the contract. I have to line up other work."

The shrill torrent of speech felt like needles going into Alida's brain. It was difficult to concentrate on what Suzanne had said, but the general thrust got through to her. Their business association had to be cut legally. Suzanne needed to be free of all obligation to her.

"Yes. Of course," she agreed jerkily.

"No!" The sharp negative from Gareth cracked around Alida like a gunshot. "There will be no signing of any release," he stated bitingly, his words obviously directed at Suzanne. "You will remain under contract for Alida Rose Creations for the full term of your commitment."

The unexpected shock of Gareth's intervention on her behalf—the savage vehemence in his voice—dazed Alida into silence.

"That's absurd!" Suzanne protested fiercely. "There'll be no income to pay my workers."

"When do you normally start production on next season's designs?" Gareth demanded.

"After the January lay-off. When the factory reopens. But you can't expect me—"

Pure steel drove Gareth's voice, cutting off Suzanne's speech. "I expect you to hold yourself and factory workers ready to produce Alida's designs when she's ready. If there's any shortfall in income due to you from the contract, it will be made good. I personally guarantee it. My solicitor will be in touch with you to that effect. Now if you don't mind letting yourself out, I'd like to be alone with my wife."

Alida could only imagine what happened next, because nothing more was said. Suzanne was apparently intimidated into submission. Alida heard her skirt around them in taking her leave. As for Gareth, she sensed an explosive tension in him, as though he was full of violent fury.

She didn't understand it. Nor did she see any sense in holding Suzanne to a business contract that couldn't be fulfilled. She heard the door click open. The need to settle things more amicably made her swivel toward it.

"No, wait!" she called. "I don't want..." In stepping away from Gareth and toward her old friend, Alida's foot caught on something. Unable to see to grasp any saving support, she flailed wildly as she fell, knocking over something else as she tumbled to the floor.

"God damn you! Get out!" Gareth yelled, and then he was gathering Alida up in his arms, carrying her. He lowered her onto what felt like a leather lounge and anxiously stroked her hair from her face. "Alida, Alida..." His voice was a rasp of deep concern.

The pain in her head was excruciating, but she reached out to him in urgent pleading. "Get Suzanne back, Gareth. I'll sign the release if she has it with her."

"No! She didn't care about you, Alida. She was only thinking of herself. I'll be damned if I'll let her close off that option for you," he replied with passionate vehemence.

Alida's hand scrabbled across his heaving chest, not understanding why he had done what he'd done, nor the reason for the turbulent vibrations emanating from him. "Gareth, Suzanne was frightened about her future. I know how that feels. And she was right. My designing days are finished."

"No, they're not!" he denied. His hands cupped her face, his fingers stroking soft persuasion. "Your sight could come back. I won't let her or anyone else take away your opportunity to follow up on the success you've had."

"And if my sight doesn't come back?"

"You could try doing it in your mind," Gareth suggested, his voice harsh with determination. "Because you can't see doesn't mean you've lost your sense of artistry. Or your memory. You said it was an expression of your life, Alida."

"But drawing—"

"Ivan Poletti can find a design student for you. Someone who can transfer your vision onto paper and sort out fabrics for you to use. Perhaps with a view to a partnership. You're strong, Alida. You don't want to give up, do you? You'd like to try it, wouldn't you? Maybe even I can help."

The pain was too bad for her to think straight any more. Nothing was making sense. "You don't like fashion, Gareth. Why are you arguing for it when you must prefer me to put it aside?"

He didn't answer immediately. One of his hands moved to gently stroke her cheek. When he did speak, his voice was low, as though scraped from deeply bedded emotion. "I want you to be happy. Whatever it takes to make you happy, I'll give it to you, Alida."

Not even the pain in her head could stop the instant welling of her emotional response. "I want you to be happy with me, Gareth," she said huskily.

"I am."

She felt his chest bend toward her and then his lips were brushing over hers. Alida closed her eyes and willed the pain away. This was too precious a moment for her to lose even the slightest nuance of the feeling that she sensed coming from Gareth. It was different to anything he had shown before. He kissed her softly, lingeringly, as though passionate desire had no place at all in their relationship.

She heard him heave a deep sigh as he lifted his mouth from hers. He traced her lips with feather-soft fingertips. "You asked me once if I loved you," he said huskily. "Well, I do. I love you, Alida Rose."

He meant it. She could feel it. All she had craved for in the long years of separation and loneliness. He gently kissed her eyelids, sweet healing balm for the pain she had suffered through him. And somehow the pain behind her eyes seemed to melt away as Gareth continued to reveal his heart to her.

"I know you think we met again by accident. And so we did. But if we hadn't met that night, the memory of you would have drawn me to find you sooner or later, Alida. I wish... But I couldn't do any other than I did. I'll make it up to you, my darling. I swear I will. And to Andy, too. Please say you understand."

"Yes," she whispered, and finally spoke the truth of her own heart. "I love you, too, Gareth. I always have. I always will. You were the man I wanted to marry. Only you, Gareth. There never was anyone else."

"Dear God!" he breathed. "How can you forgive me, everything I've done?"

"Because I want you so much," she confessed, and buried her face in his throat, luxuriating in the warmth pulsing from him, the love that had been locked away from her until now.

His arms tightened around her. A hand worked through her long hair, moving haphazardly, kneading, stroking, reflecting the disturbance of his thoughts. "What can I say to you?" he murmured in anguish. "I had to deny you, Alida. And you were right. I did form an image of you that I could deny. What I felt for you—it was so disloyal to Kate. But it tore me apart having to let you go. I couldn't let you go a second time, Alida. Even though you hated me, I couldn't let you go."

He trailed soft yearning kisses over her hair. "These weeks of waiting, being with you, realising what I really felt but sensing all your deep reservations about me. I didn't know how to break them down, Alida. I thought you'd never come to trust me. I hoped that when I had you to myself at Riordan River, maybe then I could get back what I'd lost there five years ago."

Alida's concern about his first marriage faded away. There would be no ghost of Kate at Riordan River. She had had her time. And that had been right, too. Alida knew in her heart that she would not have respected Gareth if he had not stood by his wife as he had promised her. Kate had been given her full due and was now laid to rest for all of them. Even Stacey.

"You are the magic of my life, Alida." Gareth's voice vibrated through her like a hum of harps at the gates of paradise. "Blind or not, it makes no difference. Say you believe me."

The hand woven through her hair gently urged her head back. He needed to see the belief written on her face. She opened her eyes, knowing they were lit from within by the burning brilliance of her love for him, no matter how sightless they were.

At first she couldn't believe what she was seeing. Light, shape, colour! Actually seeing! She lifted a hand to his cheek, touching the visible line of it as his other features became more discernible, clear.

Her heart beat a wild paean of joy as she saw the anguished loving in his eyes, such beautiful expressive blue eyes.

"Gareth!" It was an ecstatic gasp. "I can see! I can see again! And I do believe you. I believed you yesterday when you said I could trust you. I believe you now. Believe me, too, Gareth."

"You can see?" The incredulous leap of joy on his face increased the excitement of the miracle.

"Yes. Yes. And the pain is gone."

"What pain?"

"In my head. Behind my eyes. It's been terrible since last night."

"That's what the specialist said," Gareth said triumphantly. "In a delayed case like yours, the return of vision is often preceded by a severe headache."

She hadn't heard that. She remembered she had stopped listening. If only she had taken notice she would have known what might be happening. But it didn't matter now. "I can see!" She laughed.

Gareth laughed, too, hauling her off the lounge and whirling her around in a wild burst of happiness before clamping her body to his in possessive caution. "I'm mad. I've got to take care of you. Maybe we should call the specialist."

"No. Not today, Gareth. Maybe tomorrow. This time is ours."

He dragged in a deep breath and released it with tremulous feeling. "At least I did right in holding off Suzanne's action."

She shook her head, smiling at him with all the confidence of love given and returned. "I don't want that life any more. I love your kind of life, Gareth."

"You mean that?" Hope warred with caution in his eyes.

"With all my heart. One day, when we've had all the children you want, I might take up painting. Jill once told me that Outback scenes sell well."

A glorious happiness danced at her. "I'll buy you all the paints and canvases you could ever use."

"And Ivan will hang them in his shop."

"And Jill will put an outrageous price on them."

"And our children—"

"Will be very proud of their mother."

"And their father." Her green eyes shone more brightly than the emerald on her finger. "Oh, Gareth! It's not a dream, is it?"

"No, my darling, it's real. Thank God it's real!"

He kissed her with such fervour that all Alida's nightmares were banished to the dim dark past. There was so much more she could tell him, but it wasn't necessary right now, and the bond they shared went beyond words, anyway.

He felt it, too.

Gareth . . . her husband.

Who loved her.

"We should go and tell our family," she murmured.

"Not yet." He smiled at her, his eyes glowing with love and the need to express it. "This wedding is ours, Alida Rose."

He was right. Their family could wait a while. The business with Suzanne could wait a while. All the good news could wait a while. This was her true wedding to Gareth Morgan, just the two of them, together in everything.

And when they kissed again there was passion as well as love, a passion that had waited five long years to be fully realised and expressed. And Alida knew, beyond a shadow of doubt, that it would last their whole lifetime.

WORDFIND #1

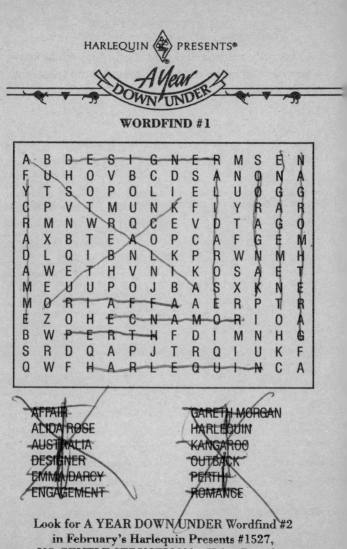

```
A B D E S I G N E R M S E N
F U H O V B C D S A N O N A
Y T S O P O L I E L U O G G
C P V T M U N K F L Y R A R
R M N W R Q C E V D T A G O
A X B T E A O P C A F G E M
D L Q I B N L K P R W N M H
A W E T H V N I K O S A E T
M E U U P O J B A S X K N E
M O R I A F F A A E R P T R
E Z O H E C N A M O R I O A
B W P E R T H F D I M N H G
S R D Q A P J T R Q I U K F
Q W F H A R L E Q U I N C A
```

AFFAIR
ALIDA ROSE
AUSTRALIA
DESIGNER
EMMA DARCY
ENGAGEMENT

GARETH MORGAN
HARLEQUIN
KANGAROO
OUTBACK
PERTH
ROMANCE

Look for A YEAR DOWN UNDER Wordfind #2
in February's Harlequin Presents #1527,
NO GENTLE SEDUCTION by Helen Bianchin

WF1

HARLEQUIN ® PRESENTS®

A Year DOWN UNDER

In February, we will take you to Sydney, Australia, with
NO GENTLE SEDUCTION by Helen Bianchin,
Harlequin Presents #1527.

Lexi Harrison and Georg Nicolaos move in the right
circles. Lexi's a model and Georg is a wealthy Sydney
businessman. Life seems perfect... so why have they
agreed to a *pretend* engagement?

Share the adventure—and the romance—
of A Year Down Under!

SOLUTIONS TO
WORDFIND #1

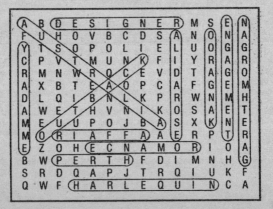

YDUJ-AR